LOS CAIDOS: THE FALLEN

To Michael (Denslow).

With best wishes and a grin. This is just about all I can do. Hope you like it.

from Michael (Barclay)
aka MICH

LOS CAIDOS: THE FALLEN

A NOVEL

M R BARCLAY

Copyright © M R Barclay 2016

M R Barclay has asserted his moral right under the Copyright, Designs and Patents Act, 1998, to be identified as the author of this work.

All rights reserved. This book is copyright material and must not be copied, reproduced, transferred, distributed, leased, licensed or publicly performed or used in any way except as specifically permitted in writing by the publisher, as allowed under the terms and conditions under which it was purchased or as strictly permitted by applicable copyright law. Any unauthorised distribution or use of this text may be a direct infringement of the author's and publisher's rights, and those responsible may be liable in law accordingly.

A catalogue record for this book is available from the British Library

Hardback edition: ISBN 978-0-9935220-0-0

Ebook edition: ISBN 978-0-9935220-1-7

First published 2016
MRB, Cornwall

Printed and bound in Great Britain by
TJ International, Cornwall

For those who waited so long.

Man is born free and everywhere he is in chains.
Jean Jacques Rousseau.

CHAPTER ONE

(1)

Ramón looked up at the statue of the angel and the man. The angel stood behind the man, a poet, its wings curving upwards towards the sky. The day was hot and white clouds drifted slowly by overhead. It was strangely quiet after the disturbances of the previous few days. Even the National Guard seemed, like the lizards, to be basking in the sun. He stole a sideways glance at the group of soldiers lounging on the far side of the square. Their leather boots and belts gleamed in the sunlight. They looked well fed and dangerous. He moved on, wishing he had avoided the square. Then he saw her. She had been coming towards him, about to cross the square, when she seemed to change her mind and turn back towards the university. He had only caught a glimpse of her face but now he hurried to catch up with her. She must have heard his footsteps behind her because she turned and he saw the fear as well as the beauty in her face.

'Don't be afraid, Señorita,' he said. 'I hate them too.' He saw her eyes stray past his shoulder as he spoke.

'I don't know what you mean, and anyway I don't know you.' Her voice was soft with the inflection of the highland region.

He fell in beside her. 'My name is Ramón. I'm a student here,' he told her.

'There are lots of students here and many are government spies,' she retorted. 'If I were you I wouldn't go about talking like that.'

'But you know I'm not a government spy.'

'How can I know that? I know nothing about you. I've never seen you before. Go away, leave me alone.'

He was aware of the soldiers watching them as they left the square. 'That's not very friendly,' he said.

'And you're not very polite.'

'I'm sorry. I didn't mean to frighten you; to offend you. Forgive me.' From behind them came the sound of a Jeep starting up. 'Don't look back.'

'I wasn't going to.' Together they began to walk towards the university. Behind them the Jeep turned into the Calle de los Mártires.

'Take hold of my hand.' He sensed her hesitation. 'Quick, do it!' The Jeep was coming up behind them. 'What's your name?'

'María.'

'María, you've got beautiful eyes.' The Jeep drew level with them. There were three soldiers in it, one in the front beside the driver, the third in the back, his M16 pointing at them over the side of the vehicle. Slowly the vehicle pulled ahead of them, the soldier in the back, stared hard at them before turning away. 'Pig,' muttered Ramón.

'Careful!' María squeezed his hand. 'Please be careful. They're just looking for an excuse to do something. Yesterday in the Calle de San Jorge they almost beat a man to death for leaving some flowers beside the road. They could kill you if you so much as look at them too long.'

Ramón looked at her in surprise. 'They wouldn't dare.'

'They shot nearly a hundred people in the Plaza de los Astros on Monday.'

'That was different. There was an anti-government demonstration going on,' he said.

'They were just ordinary people!' Ramón was surprised by the passion in her voice but before he could think of a reply she said, 'OK there was a lot of shouting and waving banners but the National Guard just opened fire.'

'They were fired on first.'

'That's nonsense! Who told you that?' she asked.

'It was on the news.'

'It isn't true. I was there. I saw what happened.'

Ramón stopped and stared at her in amazement. 'You were in the Plaza de los Astros?'

'Keep walking, people may be looking at us and please don't talk so loudly.'

Ramón looked at the people nearest them but as far as he could tell none of them seemed unduly interested in either María or him. Lowering his voice, he said, 'Tell me what happened? Why did they open fire and what were you doing there?'

'Everybody I know was there. It was no different from the demonstration last week, just a lot bigger. There were too many of us for them to beat up, so they just shot into the crowd.'

'On the television they said that the rebels had come into the city and opened fire on the troops from behind the crowd.'

'That isn't true.'

'So, what happened?' he asked.

She glanced round them before answering. 'The National Guard must have just decided to break up the demonstration. At first I thought they were firing into the air but as the crowd began to panic, I saw some people on the ground. You could tell they had been shot; they were laying there, sort of crumpled up, untidy looking. Everybody was trying to get out of the square but the soldiers kept shooting. We could hear it as we ran down the Calle de San Juan. A man near me had been hit; he was covered in blood. It was terrifying. I don't think I've ever felt so scared in all my life.'

In front of them the Jeep turned right out of the Calle de los Mártires. María let out an audible sigh of relief. 'Thank God they're gone.'

'They won't be far away.'

'They're never far away.' As if to emphasise the point

the noise of gunfire suddenly sounded from across the city. Ramón and María looked at one another.

He said, 'You really do have the most beautiful eyes.'

She smiled for the first time. 'Thank you Señor, you are too kind.' They both laughed. 'No seriously, thank you for what you did back there; for giving me courage.'

'For giving you courage? I don't understand.'

'It doesn't matter.' She was still smiling at him.

Ramón said, 'So you no longer think me impolite?'

'I think you are very impolite but I know you are not a government spy.'

'No, I'm not a government spy.'

'So what are you?'

'I told you; I'm a student.'

'A student of what?'

'Of law.'

'A student of law. A student of law, here, in this country!'

'Yes, why not?'

She knew she had offended him. 'I'm sorry, I didn't mean to be rude.' She saw the doubt in his eyes. 'No, I mean it. It's just that there is no law here. You must know that.'

'These are difficult times,' he replied.

María looked at him closely. 'What made you choose law?' she asked.

'Law is important. Without law there can be no justice. Without justice there can be no freedom. Law is the foundation stone of society. Besides,' he added self-consciously, 'my father is an advocate. It sort of runs in the family.'

They were nearing the intersection with the Via de la República. María said, 'I have to see somebody. I'm already late. They may be worrying about me.'

'Your man? I'm sorry; it's not really my business but I'd like to see you again.' He did not want this girl to just pass out of his life. 'Already you seem to know all about me,' he continued, 'I hardly know anything about you.'

'I'd like to see you again too,' she replied. 'No, the person I have to see is not my man. I have no man, as you put it.'

She was smiling at him again. Ramón smiled back. 'I'm glad,' he said. 'Where shall we meet? When?'

'How about the same time the day after tomorrow, outside the Church of Our Lady of Mercy? There will be lots of people and everybody will have a reason for being there. We will not attract the attention of the National Guard.'

'Fine, I'll be there.' She really is afraid of them, he thought. 'See you then,' he said.

'See you then,' she replied. 'Vaya con Dios.' With that she turned and walked quickly away along the Via de la República.

Ramón watched her go. May God go with you too, he thought. He noticed the faint swing of her hips, the shapeliness of her legs and he offered up a silent prayer of thanks that somehow, uncharacteristically, he had found himself able to just approach and speak to this beautiful young woman.

(2)

The following day there was another massive demonstration in the city. The truth about the massacre in the Plaza de los Astros had become widely known despite continuous radio and television reports claiming that the National Guard had come under attack. People flocked onto the streets in their thousands. Banners again calling for the resignation of the president and the holding of fresh elections appeared alongside others demanding justice for Monday's dead. Slogans daubed overnight on the walls of the capital were everywhere. Across the front of the Banco Nacional someone had scrawled, *'The nation's wealth belongs to the people, not to foreign investors!'* The National Guard, seemingly taken by surprise by this reaction, remained in their barracks.

As Ramón made his way along the Avenida de la Democracia everyone appeared to be drifting towards the Plaza de los Astros, as if the absence of the National Guard, usually so much in evidence, had created a vacuum at the city's centre into which all were being drawn with the inevitability of scientific law. Among the crowd he noticed many obviously middle class city dwellers shoulder to shoulder with campesinos presumably from the surrounding countryside. Strangely the atmosphere seemed excited rather than angry and Ramón found himself hoping that the president would at least respond by having those members of the army responsible for Monday's bloodshed brought to trial. Most of the crowd, however, seemed as concerned about having fresh elections and Ramón wondered to whom their appeals were addressed. He also wondered if the rebels had indeed entered the city, as the government was claiming.

As he approached the Plaza de los Astros he noticed a bunch of flowers beside the wall of the Consolidated Mines building and a line of bullet holes at chest height above them. There were eight small craters, each with hairline cracks radiating out from them across the face of the stonework. He suddenly found himself thinking of María and how any human being could be alive one moment and lying inert and lifeless the next, crushed like an insect beneath the sole of a shoe. A boot might be more appropriate, he thought grimly to himself. The National Guard seemed to be becoming more and more like the Brigadas Especiales, with little or no respect for human life or the law.

Ramón walked past three similar pathetic reminders of lives suddenly brought to an abrupt end, and on into the square. He remembered what María had told him about the National Guard having beaten a man virtually to death for having left a few flowers where someone had been killed. It might have been for his son or even his wife; any friend or relative, it made no difference to the army. On several occasions Ramón had seen campesinos being dragged away by soldiers. He had assumed they must be troublemakers, agitators, people who in some way posed a threat to the state. But what was the threat in leaving a few flowers where someone had died? What had become of the law, the foundation stone of society? It occurred to him that for some time now the army and especially the Brigadas Especiales Contra Actos de Terrorismo, seemed less and less to be upholding the law, as reducing it to a meaningless series of statutes that had little or nothing to do with the real world. Deeply troubled, he moved among the crowd like a man looking for something he had lost.

Beside the statue of the angel he stopped to listen to a man who was addressing the crowd from the steps of the National Theatre. 'The foreign aid never reached the earthquake victims,' the man was saying, 'the earthquake was three years ago; who among you ever received a thing?' he paused. The whole crowd stood in silence as if awaiting the sacrament. 'Nobody here? Then perhaps you know of someone who did?' Again the speaker paused and again the crowd remained silent as if the whole of the Plaza de los Astros was filled with one congregation, a congregation of the dispossessed.

Ramón looked at the people nearest him. The faces of the campesinos were like weathered masks, impassive. If these are the meek of the earth, he thought, I would not like to be among the ungodly when their time comes.

'Look around you,' the speaker enjoined the crowd. 'Look at this country of ours. What do you see? I'll tell you what you see. You see the few riding on the backs of many. That is what you see.'

The appeal to envy, thought Ramón, but is it? Most of his fellow countrymen lived miserable lives in squalid conditions. He did not know what had happened to the foreign aid the speaker was referring to. He had been eighteen when the earthquake struck but while it was obvious that part of the city had already been rebuilt, many people still remained virtually homeless, living in the so-called shantytowns on the outskirts of the city. The beautiful new Teatro Nacional probably did not mean much to them.

'The money went into the pockets of the rich,' the speaker continued, 'into the pockets of the bosses. The earthquake was no disaster for them, they grew even richer rebuilding the city.'

He could well be right about that, thought Ramón. There were constant rumours of corruption surrounding government contracts. Similarly, the great influx of foreign investment that the government kept boasting about did not seem to bring much benefit to the lives of the majority and he for one was glad he did not have to work in the silver mines. Stories of the appalling conditions in which men were forced to work seemed, if true, a terrible price to pay for wages that were only marginally better than those of the coffee pickers.

Ramón began to move away. I must tell Father about the slogan on the wall of the Banco Nacional, he thought. Behind him he heard the speaker say, 'This government is a government of the rich for the rich. This government is the government of the bosses. This government is evil and corrupt and must be swept away!'

Ramón was not sure whether he despised the speaker or felt a certain admiration for the man. What he said sounded too much like rebel propaganda but in parts at least it had the ring of truth. The man himself was either very stupid or very brave. As from today he would be a marked man. The army might not be on the streets but that was not to say that their spies were not. The president might move to curb the worst excesses of the army, if for no other reason than that the foreign press might pick up the story of Monday's massacre. He might even agree to fresh elections, though Ramón doubted it, but if this man ever fell into his hands he would never be seen again. People were rumoured to have disappeared for far less. As for the National Guard, they were now universally despised. Ramón had even heard one of his father's friends say they were the rebels' best recruiting agent.

(3)

'That's all very well my boy,' his father said. Luis Rodrigo was a man of nearly fifty. Though not a tall man, he was nevertheless an imposing one. A successful advocate with a jovial sense of humour he was proud of his wife and they got on well together. Angelina Rodrigo was by contrast a tall and angular woman of a rather startling beauty. Ten years younger than her husband she was capable of an incisiveness that sometimes took her husband by surprise. Ramón was their only child and in both looks and temperament tended to take after his mother.

The three of them were at dinner in the family town home, a spacious airy building surrounded by a walled garden that wrapped the house in a blanket of stillness and muted the city's noise. 'That's all very well,' Luis Rodrigo said, 'but what exactly does it mean? It's like all this Marxist nonsense, it sounds wonderful but means nothing. What wealth? We have no wealth. Without foreign investment there would be no development. Foreign investment is what this country needs to drag it into the twentieth century.'

'I wasn't defending it Father, I just saw it written up across the wall of the Banco Nacional that's all.'

'Disgraceful, whatever next.'

'Mind you,' Ramón added as if as an after-thought, 'I do think it contains an element of truth.' Out of the corner of his eye he noticed his mother's slight smile.

'Oh, you do, do you?' Luis Rodrigo looked thoughtfully at his son. 'Then perhaps you would care to tell us what that is?'

Ramón turned his wine glass in his hand. 'Well, anyone can attract foreign investment at a price,' he replied.

'Go on,' Luis Rodrigo invited his son.

Angelina Rodrigo observed their game in amused silence. 'Well,' continued Ramón, 'you agree that investment goes where there's the opportunity to make a profit?'

'Well, of course I agree. That's what business is all about. That's why people invest in anything, to make a profit. The whole world's monetary order is based on the same principle.'

'Yes, but,' Ramón replied, 'if a government sells off mineral rights to foreign companies at ludicrously low prices for example, it will attract foreign investors all right but who gains other than the foreign companies who exploit that opportunity? Not the citizens of that country. They've been sold short. Effectively they have been robbed.'

'Are you suggesting that's what's happened in this country?' his father asked.

'Well the only people who seem to make anything from the silver mines apart from the government who sold the leases, are the foreign owners. The poor devils who work in them certainly aren't making much.'

'They get the going rate.'

'Yes but who fixed that rate? Come on, Father, you know as well as I do that the vast majority of the people in this country live in conditions of appalling poverty and that also includes those who are working for precisely those foreign companies who were persuaded to invest here.'

'One of the reasons those foreign companies were persuaded to come here,' Luis Rodrigo replied, 'was because labour costs were comparatively low. The government cannot just snap its fingers and expect foreign companies to come running. They're not charities. They come because there's opportunity here. Better opportunity here, than elsewhere. The government's job is to ensure political stability and try to get the best deal it can.'

'But the best deal for whom?'

'Well for the country of course,' Luis Rodrigo snapped.

Angelina Rodrigo decided it was time to intervene. 'Now stop it you two,' she said. 'Must we discuss politics at the dinner table?'

Luis Rodrigo looked at his wife and his sense of irritation passed. 'I'm sorry my dear.' Turning to his son he said, 'Your mother is quite right. Politics isn't a fit topic of conversation for the dinner table.'

'Mother, how can you just dismiss what is happening all around us as unfit for discussion just because we happen to be having dinner?' asked Ramón in exasperation.

Just then the maid entered the room with the main course. 'It's not always wise to speak of these things,' Angelina replied. 'Your grandfather ended up getting shot for dabbling in politics.'

'That's hardly the same as discussing current affairs at one's own dinner table.'

'Ramón!' Luis Rodrigo put down his glass. 'I will not have you speaking to your mother like that. Apologise immediately.'

'Hush, Luis.' Angelina placed her hand upon her husband's arm. 'Ramón didn't mean to be rude, did you Ramón?'

'Of course not Mother.'

'I'm glad to hear it, young man,' his father said, though he wondered if his son had begun mixing with the wrong sort of people at the university.

'I just don't see why we can't talk about what is going on in our country just because we happen to be at the dinner table,' replied Ramón.

'Well let us talk about it if we must,' his mother said, 'but I do hope you aren't going to let politics get in the way of your studies, that's all.'

'Of course not Mother, but I am supposed to be studying law, remember.'

'I don't see why your studies demand that you attend political demonstrations,' Angelina Rodrigo replied.

'That's hardly fair my dear,' Luis said. 'The boy was on his way home.'

'I wish you'd stop calling me a boy, Father. I'm nearly twenty two.'

'Yes of course you are son. I'm sorry. Just a habit.'

For a while they ate their dinner in silence. Eventually Luis Rodrigo said, 'That was really a rather good wine, don't you think?'

'Oh really dear! When you try being diplomatic you remind me of an elephant trying to tiptoe through a china shop.' They all laughed.

'You should see me in court sometimes.'

'Have they thrown you any buns yet Father?'

'Not yet, but anything is possible in these times.'

'Is that a political statement?' asked Ramón.

'Oh really, you two!' Angelina looked from one to the other. 'I don't know which of you is worse.' Sometimes they are so alike, she thought. 'You shouldn't encourage him Luis.'

'Me! What did I do?' Luis looked at his wife, an expression of comic surprise on his face.

'Isn't that what the accused usually say?' observed Ramón.

'If you were listening carefully my boy, you would realise that I am the accused.' The room was again filled with their laughter.

The dinner drew to an agreeable end and the family moved to the drawing room. The television news announced a dusk to dawn curfew to come into effect the following evening. Only brief mention was made of the demonstration in the Plaza de los Astros.

'At least no one was killed this time,' Angelina said. Outside the light had begun to fade as night approached and an uneasy silence lay over the city, but the orange Jeeps of the Brigadas Especiales were again out on the streets.

(4)

After María left Ramón, she made her way to the house of Pablo Herendez, a dark and secretive man who believed that no significant change was ever brought about in society without struggle and bloodshed, and a man who took perverse pleasure when events seemed to support this view. Had he by quirk of circumstance found himself in the National Guard, he would have served it with the same ruthless determination that he now fought against it. He was a man with a limitless capacity to trade savagery for savagery, outrage for outrage and to justify this by saying that war is war. A dreamer and a strategist, he was valued by the rebels for the organisational abilities he was able to bring to the armed struggle now gaining momentum in the countryside and about to enter the cities.

María knew little of this but with intuitive insight sensed what Pablo Herendez was and secretly named him the devil's general, though later he became widely known as El Tigre de la Noche, The Tiger of the Night.

'You're late,' Pablo Herendez said when they met. He

disliked women, thinking them weak and incapable of carrying out the business of war efficiently, though he valued their expendability and appreciated their usefulness as messengers. María, however, he took an instant intense dislike to because she was so beautiful. Too beautiful to escape the notice of the National Guard and because her beauty awoke his own lust and thus exposed a weakness within himself.

'I'm sorry,' she replied, 'I was delayed.'

'What sort of an excuse do you call that?'

'It was an apology not an explanation,' she fired back.

'Clever are you, as well as pretty? Well, we'll see if we can find a use for your cleverness.'

'Must you be so offensive? I only came here because I was told to deliver this,' she handed him the envelope.

'Are you sure you weren't followed?'

'Can one ever be sure?'

'Do you know what's in this envelope?'

'Of course not. I was just told to deliver it and to ask if there was any message I should take back?'

'No message, except that you are not to come here again. They're not to send you here ever again. Do you understand?' María nodded saying nothing. 'When you leave here be careful, do not attract the attention of the National Guard'.

'I will try not to,' she replied icily. 'May I go now?'

'Yes, go.' He turned away, apparently deep in his own thoughts, oblivious to her presence.

With that María left him. She never saw him again, though she, like many others, lived through events planned by his brilliant but diabolical mind.

(5)

Ramón and María met as planned outside the church of Our Lady of Mercy. Ramón was early and though there were many people on the streets, so were the National Guard together with the much-feared Brigadas Especiales in their orange Jeeps. Eventually she appeared coming out of the church. Seeing him waiting, she gave a little wave.

'I thought you were never going to show up,' he said.
'Was I late?'
'Not really, I was early.' He watched her remove her scarf and shake her hair free. It fell black and shining onto her shoulders. He said, 'I seem to have caught your nervousness about the army. The National Guard are everywhere, just cruising about and staring at everybody.'

'Today they are but were you in the Plaza de los Astros yesterday?' she asked.

'Yes, but not for long. I was on my way home. Why, were you?'

'Yes. Wasn't it amazing? So many people were on the streets. But the most extraordinary thing of all was that representatives of the rebels openly addressed the crowd. Here in the capital.' Ramón glanced at her, but she seemed not to notice. 'That's never happened before,' she continued, 'and the National Guard were nowhere to be seen. I never thought I would live to see the day when a man stood up and publicly called the army murderers in the service of a tyrant! Thousands of people must have heard him.'

'Including many informers and members of the Special Brigades not in uniform I expect,' observed Ramón looking at the people around them.

She noticed his nervousness and her expression changed. 'Yes, I thought that too at the time,' she replied. 'He was taking a terrible risk.'

They began to descend the church steps. Ramón thought, she seems different today, more carefree. He said, 'You seem very happy today.'

'Do I?' She turned towards him and gave him a dazzling smile. 'Perhaps it's because I feel things are going to change. There are so many people wanting things to change.'

'Things will change all right,' he said, 'but not necessarily for the better.'

'Oh Ramón, don't. I always feel happier when I've been to church and I've been looking forward to seeing you again.' It was the first time she had used his name. She looked serious for a moment before the smile slowly returned.

For his part Ramón had been wondering whether she really would meet him as they had arranged. Now for a long moment they stood looking at each other, two young people recognising the mutual promise of a possible future. Then quite unselfconsciously María took hold of Ramón's hand. 'Let's go to the Park of the Apostles.'

'Good idea,' he replied.

Together they began to walk towards the park. A short burst of gunfire came from the outskirts of the city. Ramón felt María flinch. 'It's all right,' he said, 'it's right across the other side of town.'

'I know but I was feeling so happy just now,' she replied.

'Aren't you still feeling happy?'

'Yes of course but you know what I mean. The troubles seemed so far away and then suddenly there was that sound. I hate the sound of gunfire.'

'Do you have relatives in that part of town?'

'No. My parents were killed when I was seven.'

'Killed,' repeated Ramón in surprise. 'How? Why?'

For a few seconds María said nothing and Ramón was on the verge of apologising for asking, when she said, 'The village in which we lived near San José was bombed. Shortly after the bombing stopped the army came into what remained of our village and did terrible things. The soldiers took my mother away. My father was shot because he tried to stop them taking her. I never saw my mother again, her body has never been found.'

'Oh María, I'm sorry. I had no idea.'

'How could you, but you had to know sometime, I suppose.' She saw the horror on his face. 'It was all a very long time ago,' she added.

'I don't know what to say.'

'Don't say anything.' They were entering the park. 'Let's go over there, under that tree.'

They made their way to it in silence and sat down in its shade. Ramón lay back on the grass and looked up at the sky.

Following his gaze María saw a bird very high, dazzling white against the rain clouds. Then it disappeared but as it did so she noticed a second bird, though that too vanished into the same cloud.

'Did you see them?' Ramón asked.

'The birds? Yes, I saw them. Two of them.'

'Yes two of them,' he smiled at her.

They sat in silence again until eventually Ramón asked, 'Do you hate them? The army, I mean.'

'I'm not sure that hate is the right word,' she replied. 'I hate what they did, and what they continue to do, and I'm not sad when they're killed so perhaps hate *is* the right word, though I'm sad in a way because they too belong to someone's family but the National Guard are murderers. They kill innocent people.' María pulled a piece of dry grass from the parched ground. 'Whatever I think about them is not just because of what they did to my parents. Those men might be dead already. I just don't believe that the government cares what the army does and I don't think there is any hope for our country as long as a government remains in power that allows such things to go unpunished.'

'Do you actually support the rebels?' Ramón asked.

For a moment María just looked at him. Then she said, 'Let me ask you a question. Do you think this government will hold fresh elections? Do you believe that if an opposition candidate were to win, even by a massive majority, that the president would step down?'

'No probably not,' Ramón replied.

'And what about the people they killed in the Plaza de los Astros,' she continued, 'or that poor man the Guard almost beat to death on the Calle de San Jorge? Do you think anything will be done about them?' When Ramón remained silent, she said, 'So, what hope is there with a government that allows such things to happen?'

Ramón saw that the sadness was back in her eyes. 'I'm sorry,' he said, 'I shouldn't have asked you about all that.'

'No Ramón, these are the important things. As a student of law you must know this better than I. Do you remember what you said when we first met, about the law being the foundation stone of society? Do you remember what I said?'

'You said there is no law here and that I must know that.' Now it was María who remained silent. 'These are difficult times,' he said at last. It seemed that her words, like recent events, threatened everything he had always believed in. 'The government is under attack. They are afraid the rebels may soon enter the city. You cannot expect the law to function as it does in times of peace.'

'Isn't that a rather strange thing for a student of law to say?'

'I'm not defending it, just stating a fact.'

'Now you do sound like an advocate.' Ramón looked at her sharply but there was no reproach either in her voice or her smile. 'Perhaps,' she added, 'if there wasn't such injustice there wouldn't be any rebels.'

'People should still abide by the law.'

'But does the army? What kind of law exists when they are free to kill with impunity?'

Ramón noticed the emotion that had crept back into her voice. Keeping his own voice flat he said, 'The government claim they are defending society, upholding what remains of the rule of law.'

'Yes but do *you* believe that? You know what the National Guard is like. If the army is itself lawless, can it claim to be upholding the law?' The point was well made and María saw Ramón's smile of recognition. 'But anyway it's the whole apparatus of state that we're talking about. We live in a country where the president has himself elected for another six years in an election that everyone knows was a farce. Then, when people protest, they are shot! You yourself said that you doubted that the president would ever step down. So, the whole idea of elections is a sham designed to give respectability to a totally corrupt regime.'

'I agree that the election was a farce,' Ramón said slowly, 'and I don't like the National Guard, no one does, but that doesn't mean there is no law or that the people should take the law into their own hands.'

'Perhaps they feel they no longer have any choice,' she replied.

'Is that what you think?' he asked.

Their eyes met and María said, 'I've already told you, I see no hope for our country as long as this government remains in power and I don't believe we will ever become free without a struggle.'

'An armed struggle?'

'Yes Ramón.' She saw the look of shock on his face and added, 'How else will we get rid of the president, or the Special Brigades for that matter?'

Ramón looked out across the park. Sitting there in the sun, it was easy to forget about rumours of corruption or of people who just disappeared in the night, less easy to forget the ever-present National Guard who prowled the streets, the power they represented, the sense of threat.

María said, 'You're very quiet.'

Ramón looked at her, saw how worry seemed to make her face look thinner, older, changed her beauty into something more statuesque. He said, 'I was thinking that in law things are easy. It's like a game of chess. The rules limit what one can do, in a sense dictate what's right but life isn't that simple. What is right in one situation may be totally unacceptable in another.'

'I don't think life is ever simple,' replied María but she was smiling at him again, though it was the sad smile of a woman older than her years and Ramón too felt sad as he smiled back.

'You could well be right,' he said. They sat in silence for a while. At last he said, 'A lot of people are going to die.'

'A lot of people have already died and they will continue to die as long as this regime remains in power.'

'But you're talking about civil war! God alone knows what the army will do.'

'What choice is there Ramón? What choice is there?'

CHAPTER TWO

(1)

Captain Miguel Hortez hated the Special Brigades. Born the same year the general became president, he had joined the National Guard when he was eighteen. At thirty-eight years of age he had seen many changes. When the general's eldest son had stepped down from the presidency, the National Guard was feared but not, as now, despised. Miguel Hortez had, until the assumption of power by the general's second son, been proud to be a soldier. However, the last eight years had seen the increasing use of the army to crush all opposition to the government. Even the experiment with a civilian administration, following the earthquake, had done little to take the army out of politics. Indeed, any idea that it was anything other than an instrument of the president was quickly discredited by the increasing brutality of the Special Brigades, who with their own separate command structure, were responsible only to him.

Miguel Hortez had not been surprised when the people had come out onto the streets to protest at the election result. From a poor family, the captain had risen from poverty through service in the National Guard, but he remembered the hopes of a better future for the whole of the country that his father had carried with him to his grave. Hopes that were never fulfilled because they were cynically betrayed by the rich and powerful few, who ran the country for their own benefit. Privately he had much sympathy for the rebels and yet he found himself in an army that was systematically hunting them down and killing them. The taking of prisoners was not encouraged but at least they were the enemy. Where it really began to bother the captain was when he was told that it was strategically necessary to destroy whole villages in order to deny support and shelter to the rebels.

Like many the world over, he knew from personal experience the horror of war. Miguel Hortez had seen things he wished he could forget. Things he had been unable to do anything about but which he believed no professional soldier should ever do. But then the rebels had done terrible things too. He particularly remembered the mutilated bodies of some National Guardsmen, from Three Brigade, who had been killed in a rebel ambush. Sadly that discovery had preceded his platoon entering a village known to have been sympathetic to the rebels and there, as a very young soldier, he had witnessed the most savage reprisals inflicted upon the inhabitants, many of whom must have been totally innocent people. Scared and young, he had played the hardened soldier and kept his silence, weighing this against the very real courage he had also seen displayed in the face of enemy action.

Recently brutality, such as beating an old man half to death on the street, had become commonplace, as had the disappearance of people suspected of being in touch with the rebels. But it was the massacre in the Plaza de los Astros that had finally proved too much for the captain. Unlike the bombing of a village in the mountains that might well be aiding the rebels, here the army had been used to gun down civilians who were peacefully protesting about injustice and a rigged election. It was as if the government was attempting to terrify them into passive acceptance of their fate. In Captain Miguel Hortez' eyes, such events were destroying the legitimacy of the state he served. He did not know where one drew the line between a state in which there was corruption and a state that was itself corrupt but he knew that day by day his position was becoming more and more untenable and Captain Miguel Hortez was a deeply troubled man.

(2)

Colonel Raul Domingo Escobar rose from behind his desk. He was a tall thin man with greying hair and eyes that invited trust. 'I'm glad you've made your true feelings known to me, Captain,' he said as he wandered over to the window. 'There are indeed things that no soldier should ever do. We are members of a noble profession and the National Guard has a fine record of service to our country.'

He stood looking out of the window, his back to Miguel Hortez. What does this fool expect me to do, he thought. Turning away from the window he returned to his desk. 'I'll speak frankly Captain,' he said. 'I share your dislike of the Brigadas Especiales, they are bringing the whole of the army into disrepute, but we're in a difficult position. When a man is transferred to the Special Brigades he's no longer under our command. I understand that you're well aware of this and your appreciation of the wider political implications of their actions does you credit, but are you also aware of the realities of power? General Gomez is an uncle of our president and takes his orders directly from him and he alone is answerable to the president for the actions of the Special Brigades. The president, as I am sure I do not have to remind you, is head of the state we're pledged to serve. While I have every sympathy with many of the points you have made they would in some quarters be regarded as treason.' The colonel raised his left hand slightly as if to forestall objection. 'Yes Captain, treason. We are a country at war. A particularly nasty and difficult war, of which you have first-hand experience. Sometimes terrible things, even indefensible things occur and there's a sense in which none of us are blameless, yet all of us are powerless. I cannot go to the president and say I object to what the Brigadas Especiales are doing. I'd be told to concentrate on my own command, in effect, to mind my own business. It would damage my credibility and jeopardise my influence when it comes to how my own troops are used. If I were to persist I suppose I might even be relieved of my command.'

The colonel paused, the wry smile on his face strangely at odds with the sadness in his eyes. 'Above a certain level Captain, survival takes on a whole new meaning. If I'm to serve my country I must nurture my influence, play court to the politicians who are our masters and who may lack the wisdom to use the power we represent, wisely. Ours is the hand that slays and our profession, the profession of arms, brings its own sad insight. There can be no harder school. We owe a debt of honour to the dead perhaps even more than we owe obligation to the living because our wisdom, such as it is, was bought with their blood. We cannot expect our unique insight to be shared by those who lack our experience of suffering and death.'

'But Sir,' Miguel Hortez could contain himself no longer, 'General Gomez is a soldier, but the Special Brigades are behaving like gangsters and it seems to me that the poor of our country know more about suffering than the army will ever know.'

'Captain! You forget yourself.' The colonel's eyes were hard. 'I've tried to explain to you. These are difficult times. We must tread carefully. Here, strategy demands that one keeps one's powder dry.'

As Captain Miguel Hortez left the office he wondered about Colonel Escobar's sudden rage and the way he abruptly brought their meeting to an end. He had felt sure the colonel shared his opinion about the increasing unpopularity of the army and the problems this caused. Colonel Escobar had even said that the Brigadas Especiales were responsible for much of the increased tension in the city, so why had he suddenly changed his attitude and virtually thrown him out of his office? Miguel Hortez tried to hide his unease as he passed through the outer office and past the ever-watchful eyes of the colonel's personal assistant.

(3)

The capital's barracks occupied a walled area exactly six blocks square in the southern sector of the city. Beyond that on the eastern edge of this rectangle, were houses almost exclusively occupied either by the military or personnel employed by the National Guard in various back-up services. As a captain, Miguel Hortez had been eligible for one of these and in the two years that he and his wife Manolita had been living there she had turned the rather austere building into a comfortable home.

Theirs was one of the houses furthest from the camp itself, almost on the dividing line between the military area and the rest of the city and they were therefore in a street that was both busier and noisier than the houses closer to the fortified main gate of the barracks. Their house was however, like most of the rest of the city, in a street lined with trees through which the sun shone, dappling the footpath with an ever-moving pattern of light and shade. In the winter months the trees offered some relief from the sun and now with the rainy season approaching they seemed to sway in the wind as if trying to embrace the clouds and hasten the rain they promised.

Miguel Hortez walked homeward, away from the brooding silence of the parade ground, deep in his own thoughts. He did not notice either the military staff car that had turned into the Avenida Bolivar or the motorcycle that overtook it immediately after the intersection until he heard the stutter of automatic fire and the screech of brakes. Drawing his sidearm, almost at the same moment the motorcycle roared past him, he stepped out into the road, crouched slightly and fired twice. He saw the pillion fall off the back at almost the same instant that bullets began to kick up from the ground around him. As he dived back towards the footpath he was aware of the motorcycle bursting into flames as it came to rest against a tree. Looking back towards the car he saw a man lower a small automatic weapon and begin to speak to a short fat man who only now emerged from the back of the car.

Miguel Hortez checked the impulse to hurl abuse at

the two men beside the car and instead turned away and walked past the pillion who lay face up in the road and on towards the still burning motorcycle beyond him. The second man lay trapped beneath it. He too was dead. A crucifix on a piece of broken silver chain lay beside the front wheel. The smell of burnt flesh mingled with the acrid smell of burnt-out wiring. Miguel Hortez realised that both men were probably not long out of their teens. Turning back to the pillion, he picked up the Uzi machine pistol that lay beside him just as the two men from the car approached. He noticed that the taller of the two was a gringo with a thin scarred face, carrying an Ingram sub-machine gun. Holding out his free hand for the Uzi, the man said in heavily accented Spanish, 'I'll take that.'

'You nearly killed me back there.'

'You're still alive aren't you,' the man replied. 'Now give me the gun Captain.' Seeing Miguel Hortez's hesitation he added, 'This gentleman is General Gomez. I'm his personal advisor and for the record Captain, I carry the rank of Colonel.'

'That is correct Captain,' the small fat man spoke for the first time. 'No doubt you've heard of me. I'm sorry if Colonel Johnson startled you but he's really a very good shot, as indeed you also appear to be. Anyway I'm most grateful to you for your prompt action. I see that between you, you have dispatched these two pieces of trash to their Maker. Pity we didn't get either of them alive, I would like to have had a little talk with them. Still, fortunes of war, eh Captain? Fortunes of war.' General Gomez stood looking at the two dead youngsters in silence for a few moments. Then turning to Miguel Hortez he said, 'I see you're with Three Brigade based here in the city, Captain. What's your name?'

'Captain Hortez, General.'

'Well Captain Hortez, I shall commend your action personally to Colonel Escobar. As it happens I was on my way to see him. I didn't realise I was so unwelcome a visitor.' He chuckled dryly. The sound reminded Miguel Hortez of a rattlesnake. 'Still,' the general continued, 'I shall be glad to have something good to tell him. Good day to you Captain.'

'Buenas tardes, General. Thank you.'

The general began to walk back to his car saying to Colonel Johnson as he went, 'I wonder where they got that from?'

Miguel Hortez heard Colonel Johnson say, 'Probably took it from that Special Advisor we lost about a year ago, I should think Sir,' but the rest of what Colonel Johnson said was drowned out by the squeal of tyres as a Jeep from the barracks slid to a stop beside the wrecked motorcycle. Colonel Johnson turned and shouted back to Miguel Hortez, 'Tell them who we are and get them to move that rubbish, Captain.' With that he followed the general to the car.

Miguel Hortez recognised the sergeant who was first

out of the Jeep but could not remember his name. The man knew him though because he said, 'You OK Captain Hortez?'

'Yes, thank you Sergeant. Now get your men to clear up here. Oh, and by the way, that's General Gomez and his bodyguard getting into that car over there. I wouldn't approach them if I were you.' With that he began to head back towards the barracks.

As he approached the general's car he saw Colonel Johnson about to climb into the driver's seat having just laid the body of the general's driver onto the road. 'You can tell them to pick this one up too, Captain,' he said, as Miguel Hortez was about to walk past.

'I'm sure they'll do that Colonel,' he replied. He did not know what reaction he had expected but the colonel's broad grin followed his back as he walked on by.

Their exchange was not missed by General Gomez, who looked thoughtfully at the receding figure of Miguel Hortez.

(4)

Later when the captain arrived home, Manolita came out into the hall to meet him. 'How was your meeting with Colonel Escobar?' she asked, as she put her arms around his neck. Perhaps a hesitation in his response, some feminine intuition, alerted her, for she drew back. 'It was bad, wasn't it?'

'I don't know,' he replied.

'Tell me.'

'Give me that kiss first,' he said, forcing a smile. They stood in the hall in each other's arms and Miguel Hortez felt a sudden sense of panic; he had so much to lose. She would have moved away from him but he tightened his grip slightly pulling her close to him. 'Where's Jaime?'

'Asleep in the kitchen,' she replied.

He could feel the warmth of her body and smell her lovely sweet, fresh smell and he found himself wanting her. She looked up into his face. Then taking his hand she said, 'Come on.'

In the bedroom she stepped out of her dress and came close to him again. As they kissed she undid his belt. He tried to catch the gun but it dropped to the floor with a thud. Then she drew him towards the bed. He struggled out of his trousers as she kissed his neck and shoulders. Then he was on top of her. She brought her knees up and her legs around him as he entered her.

(5)

Afterwards, lying on the bed beside one another, he said, 'I've been a soldier twenty years. Soldiers see a lot of killing.' He paused, 'Sometimes do a lot of killing. It goes with the territory. It's part of the job; it's what I'm paid for.'

Manolita propped herself on one elbow and looked down at him. 'Is that what Colonel Escobar said?' There was anger in her voice. 'He had no cause to speak to you like that. You're a good soldier, the men respect you.'

'It's got nothing to do with Colonel Escobar,' he replied.

'What is it then? What's happened Miguel? Tell me.'

Reluctantly he said, 'Two youths on a motorbike tried to kill General Gomez.'

'Two youths tried to kill General Gomez,' Manolita repeated puzzled. 'When? What has this got to do with you? I don't understand. Miguel, what's happened?' Miguel Hortez swung his legs off the bed and picked up his trousers. 'Miguel?'

'It's all right Manolita, I just need time to think.'

She came round the bed and knelt in front of him. 'Don't shut me out Miguel.'

'I'm not. Believe me Lita, I'm not.' The silence yawned between them like a chasm. Into this silence he said, 'On my way home, at the intersection between Avenida Bolivar and El Paseo de Colon, two youths on a motorcycle tried to kill that bastard Gomez but instead I killed them.'

The sound of a truck in the street outside drifted into the room. From a long way away he heard Manolita ask, 'How did it happen Miguel?'

Wearily he began to tell her. He told her how the front wheel of the burnt-out motorcycle was still turning and how young the rebels had been and how the gringo advisor seemed to find it all mildly amusing. 'It all happened so fast. I didn't know who was in the car, only that it was an army vehicle. Then the motorcycle was passing me.' He paused, 'Then they were just lying there.'

The silence seemed to settle in the room. 'But they were rebels?'

'Yes.' He was not sure if it had been a question. 'Yes, they were rebels.'

'And it was General Gomez?'

'Yes, it was Gomez all right.'

'It's a pity they didn't,' Manolita began, then stopped. Their eyes met.

'Yes,' he said.

They began to get dressed. 'It wasn't your fault Miguel.' He continued dressing in silence, avoiding her eyes. 'You couldn't have known. You had to shoot.'

'I could have aimed to miss.'

'But you didn't know.'

'No, I didn't know,' he agreed. Manolita watched him as he picked up the gun. 'I could use a beer,' he said. She gave him a twitchy smile and left the room. 'I'll be there in a moment,' he called out after her. Sitting on the bed, he quickly cleaned and refilled the weapon.

When he entered the kitchen Jaime was still sleeping. Together they left him where he was and went out onto the front steps. 'Did you have your meeting with Colonel Escobar?' Manoilita asked.

When he had finished telling her about his conversation with the colonel, she said, 'Be careful Miguel. I don't think you can trust that one. He's too close to the men of power. They're all the same. If you are useful to them they are polite to you, but if you antagonise them they will remember. It could be dangerous. Personally I think that one's mad, he seems to be in love with death.'

Miguel Hortez looked at his wife and wondered how she managed to put into words what he himself half knew, but could never express.

(6)

'General Gomez, let me offer my apologies.' For once the self-assured Colonel Escobar looked slightly ill at ease. 'One of my men has already told me something of what has just occurred.'

'News travels fast it seems,' observed the general, 'but I hardly think you need apologise. I presume the two gunmen were not part of your welcome.'

'Indeed they were not General,' replied Colonel Escobar, though the thought that it was perhaps a pity they had failed passed rapidly through his mind.

'You know Colonel Johnson of course,' the general continued. The American hardly bothered to hide his contemptuous smile as Colonel Escobar inclined his head slightly in acknowledgement.

The two men had taken an instant dislike to one another. General Gomez was well aware of this but sometimes it amused him to see the way his dogs of war snarled at each other, however discreetly, but now he felt he should have denied himself the pleasure. Colonel Johnson had been out of the car long before it had come to a standstill and the man had already saved his life once before when he had been visiting troops in the Highlands. Today Johnson had again displayed the skill and ruthlessness for which he had been hired. The realisation of his own self-indulgence did little to improve the general's humour. He said, 'I didn't come here to discuss today's little drama though we may as well deal with matters arising from it now. To begin with I'll need another driver, Escobar. See to it that a man is seconded immediately. We'll give him any additional training he may need.'

Colonel Escobar had not known that the general's driver had been killed. A good driver was like gold dust and he knew he could not pass a bad one off onto General Gomez. It irked him how General Gomez and indeed the Brigadas Especiales could commandeer whatever men or material they wanted. It irked him still more to be spoken to like this in front of the gringo who seemed particularly to enjoy his humiliation. 'I'll see to it General,' he said.

'Second,' General Gomez continued, 'the fact that an attack on any military vehicle could occur so close to this base suggests a very serious lapse in security. You were no doubt aware Colonel, that the rebels were expected to try and mount an attack within the city but do you realise that, had they not been stopped, it looks very much as if they planned to ride right past the main gate! That's more than audacious Colonel, it shows a complete contempt for the National Guard.'

'With respect General, I don't,' began Colonel Escobar but the general waved him into silence.

'Which brings me to the whole question of Three Brigade's performance. I presume you ordered the troops to return to barracks Colonel?'

'I did. Yes, General.'

'Why?'

'To avoid further direct confrontation between the army and the people.'

'I see,' said the general. 'We'll return to the wisdom of that particular decision later but first I have to say that I'm not satisfied by the apparent lack of commitment of Three Brigade. My Special Forces cannot be expected to control the situation in the city if they receive virtually no support from the National Guard.'

This was too much for Colonel Escobar. He said, 'I hardly think that's fair, General. Three Brigade's job isn't made any easier by the way the Special Brigades totally alienate the civilian population!' General Gomez looked as if he were about to choke with rage but Colonel Escobar had always believed that the best form of defence was attack. If the general was going to criticise the troops under his command then he was going to hear what he, Colonel Raul Domingo Escobar, thought of the Brigadas Especiales. 'The rebels,' he continued, 'gain a sympathiser every time the Special Brigades are seen throwing their weight around, General, and today's sympathiser is tomorrow's helper.' From the corner of his eye he noticed that Colonel Johnson was no longer grinning. He pressed on, 'The audacity of today's attack should not blind us to the intelligence it presupposes. Further, this attack couldn't have taken place without at least the tacit support of many people, even if that support amounted to no more than a lot of people looking the other way.'

General Gomez's face looked as if it had been carved out of stone, only his eyes seemed to glow. Colonel Escobar had a sudden vision of the fires of hell itself raging within the general's skull, but he was surprised that it was the American who spoke.

'That's bullshit, Colonel and I'll tell you why it's bullshit. In Nam, Charlie used to go into villages and drag the headman or anyone who opposed the Cong to the stockade and impale them on it. He was then left there not just to die but to be seen dying. We never got any help from anybody in those villages, Colonel!'

'This is not Vietnam,' snarled Colonel Escobar. 'You were driven out of Vietnam remember. We need the help of the people in order to crush the rebels. We won't get that help if they all hate us. Already we've lost control of the countryside, just as you did in Vietnam.'

'It doesn't matter a damn if they hate us, you dumb bastard! What matters is that they aren't more afraid of the rebels than of us! And for the record, if we'd been given a free hand in Vietnam we'd have driven the gooks all the way back to Hanoi.'

Colonel Escobar spoke quietly but there was no mistaking the menace in his voice. 'Don't ever call me a bastard again, you gringo dog,' he said.

'That's enough!' General Gomez's voice was equally menacing. 'I decide strategy.' The two colonels glared at one another. They all became aware of the ticking of the wall clock but it was Colonel Johnson who looked up at it and then back to Colonel Escobar. The seconds continued to tick by. At length the general said, 'Neither of those two demonstrations in the Plaza de los Astros should ever have been allowed to take place. But when they did, they should have been broken up immediately before large numbers of people became involved. The moment people sense weakness they become harder to control. As the instrument of government it is our job to exercise control. We do not do that by asking the people to disperse Colonel, we tell them. If they do not obey, we shoot them.'

'I have shot many men, General,' said Colonel Escobar.

'I do not doubt it, Colonel,' replied the general, 'but

what we are discussing is the best way to maintain order within the city.'

Colonel Johnson said, 'Well you already know my view General.'

'While I have little sympathy for Colonel Escobar's view,' replied General Gomez, 'in this case Colonel, I don't think we should do anything to publicise this attack.'

'They were killed, General. We lost no men or material.'

'But it hardly shows us in a good light. The rebels may be seen as men of daring. There may be those who would be encouraged to lend them their support.'

'They'll side sooner or later anyway, General.'

'But with us, hopefully,' replied General Gomez.

'And do you think,' asked Colonel Escobar, 'that opening fire on the crowd in the Plaza de los Astros won any hearts and minds, General?'

'That's insubordination, Colonel.'

'It was a question, General.'

For several seconds General Gomez looked at him in silence. Then he said, 'Men of the Brigadas Especiales opened fire because they were carrying out my direct orders. Those orders were to put some backbone into the garrison troops and let the people know that civil disorder will not be tolerated. Their action reflected a strategic decision, Colonel. Such decisions are made either by the president or myself. Do you question that decision?'

Colonel Escobar was not in the mood for caution. He said, 'Its wisdom yes. I do not question orders General, but as the garrison commander, why was I not made aware of that decision?'

'Because,' roared the general, 'I'm not answerable to you!'

Colonel Escobar knew that he had placed himself in jeopardy. He also knew that the danger, though different, was probably greater than any he had faced on the field of battle. He realised that it had been the gringo who had triggered his anger and that this had impaired his judgement. He decided that, should the opportunity ever arise, he would kill the American.

'If it wasn't for your previous record Escobar,' the general's voice sounded hoarse, 'I would seriously consider recommending to the president that you be relieved of your command.' He coughed and spat on the floor of the colonel's office. The fury that briefly contorted his face had passed, leaving it even more of a mask than before. It was if a fire had swept across the earth leaving it charred and lifeless. 'I was in León at the time of the disturbances there,' the general continued. 'They were easily put down. The mistake that was made here was that not enough people were shot during the first demonstration! If they had realised that civil disturbance will be met with an iron fist there wouldn't have been a second demonstration.' The general stopped speaking. Colonel Escobar remained silent. 'You have nothing to say, Colonel?'

'What can I say, General? As the officer commanding, I made an operational decision. I have told you why I made that decision. You apparently consider that decision to have been a mistake.'

The abruptness with which Colonel Escobar stopped speaking allowed the sound of a platoon of soldiers marching across the parade ground to enter the room. Into this silence the general said, 'It *was* a mistake, Colonel.' The words settled like a vulture onto a corpse.

'As you say, General,' replied Colonel Escobar but he looked the general straight in the eye as he said it.

After General Gomez and Colonel Johnson had gone, Colonel Escobar returned to his office where he smashed his fist into the wall so hard that a glass-encased photograph of the president that hung close by, dropped to ground and smashed. Rubbing his bruised knuckle he looked down at the remains and began to laugh.

CHAPTER THREE

(1)

A day had passed since the second demonstration in the Plaza de los Astros. The city seemed to be holding its breath. Instead of the people coming out onto the streets again, as might have been expected, everything seemed to have returned to normal. It was as if the second demonstration had been some sort of collective dream, a flower of the imagination, a psychological projection of the people's wish for freedom that had somehow strayed into the real world. Just as the city waited for the ever increasing rain clouds to release their much-needed rain, so the people waited, hoping for the annulment of the election and an announcement by the president that those responsible for the massacre in the Plaza de los Astros would be brought to justice. They waited in vain.

That night, the first night of the curfew, the army opened fire on a group of people who were slow in getting off the street. Three were killed including a young woman only recently married. News of this spread like wildfire and with it a new mood of defiance replaced the optimism that had preceded it.

The next day, small groups of people kept forming in the plazas and at the intersections of the city but these usually just melted away at the first sign of the orange Jeeps of the Brigadas Especiales, now invariably accompanied by a truckload of heavily armed soldiers. In the early evening, however, an hour before the curfew, one such group were fired upon in the Plaza de Aragón killing one man and wounding three others. The National Guard took the wounded away but left the dead man lying in the street. At about the same time as this occurred, rumours of the attempt on the life of General Gomez began to circulate throughout the city. Many who, before these latest shootings would have deplored such an attack, secretly rejoiced that someone had tried to rid the country of this man while at the same time mourning the death of the two young men whose lives had been lost in the attempt. Overnight they became heroes of the revolution, the latest anonymous martyrs to freedom in a country of martyrs and of dreams.

In the Rodrigo family it was Ramón who first heard the news of the attempt on the general's life. On the university campus the students were, since the massacre in the Plaza de los Astros, nearly all rebel sympathisers and, whereas before, all political discussions had taken place in small groups and only between trusted friends, now the attack on General Gomez was being openly discussed. Since meeting María, however, Ramón had begun keeping his thoughts to himself. When a friend observed that he seemed rather quiet and withdrawn, Ramón had merely replied that he was worried by the deteriorating political situation and the possible consequences of the attack on General Gomez. His friend had laughed and said it was more likely to be because he was in love. However, the general air of excitement in the university contrasted sharply with his own grim feelings of foreboding.

(2)

Luis Rodrigo was standing by the window of the lounge with his usual evening drink in his hand when Ramón entered the room. 'Someone tried to kill General Gomez,' he said.

'Would it be too much to ask for the usual civilised courtesies to be observed rather than have you come bursting into the room announcing that someone tried to kill someone else?' Luis Rodrigo turned back to the window.

'I'm sorry. Good evening, Father.' He paused and, as his father remained silent, added, 'Two men on a motorbike tried to shoot General Gomez earlier today.'

Luis Rodrigo turned reluctantly away from contemplating the garden and eyed his son with distaste. 'And where did you hear that piece of gossip?' he asked. 'Apart from the fact that it's almost certainly nonsense, I fail to understand why the idea should afford you such obvious pleasure! Since when did the law and those who practice it, or indeed aspire to practice it, take pleasure in murder or attempted murder?'

'For God's sake, Father, you're not in court now!'

'And do not speak to me in that manner either, young man! I don't know what's got into you recently. The other day at dinner you were rude to your mother and now you just come bursting in here and…'

'Father, I just wanted to tell you that someone tried to kill General Gomez. You know General Gomez, the president's security chief and the man who is directly responsible for the Special Brigades.'

'I know who General Gomez is!' thundered his father, now really angry.

'I don't know what's got into you,' began Ramón.

'You don't know,' spluttered his father. 'How dare you!'

'What is all this shouting about?' Angelina Rodrigo's appearance could hardly have come at a more opportune time. 'Luis?' As neither of them answered she said, 'May I too have a drink?'

'Yes of course, my dear,'

As Luis walked to the drinks cabinet, Ramón said, 'What's the matter with Father? All I did was tell him that someone tried to shoot General Gomez and he jumped down my throat.'

'Is this true, Luis?'

'Is what true, my dear?'

'That someone tried to kill General Gomez of course,' replied Angelina.

'How should I know? Ask the boy.'

'Luis!'

Luis Rodrigo looked at his wife. Her calmness seemed to bring the promise of sanity to a world crumbling into chaos. 'I'm sorry,' he said and meant it.

'There's enough trouble in the world without you two snarling at each other like a pair of stray dogs.' She took the glass he offered her. Turning to Ramón she said, 'Now what's all this about? Has someone really killed General Gomez?'

'They tried to kill him, yes. Everyone at the university was talking about it.'

Despite himself his father said, 'And that makes it true of course?'

'All right it isn't true!' retorted Ramón.

Angelina Rodrigo looked from one to the other. This is not like them, she thought. Usually theirs was a playful banter full of humour and wit. She said, 'Why do you doubt the truth of this, Luis?'

'It's not that I doubt the truth of these rumours. It's the fact that they are just rumours,' he replied. 'The city is full of rumours.'

'Would you rather I'd come home and said absolutely nothing about it when everyone else in the city is talking about nothing else?' asked Ramón.

Luis Rodrigo was aware of his wife's gaze. 'No of course not.' Then turning to his wife he said, 'Every day there are stories of people being shot or just disappearing. These undermine public confidence in the rule of law.'

'What rule of law, Father?'

'Quietly Ramón.' Angelina's own voice was soft.

'What rule of law?' Ramón repeated.

Angelina Rodrigo saw the haunted look in her husband's eyes and suddenly she understood the reason for it. She said, 'Ramón can't you see that your father is worried?'

'Why take it out on me?'

'I'm sure your father didn't mean to take it out on you, as you put it,' replied his mother. 'Now come you two, don't make me sad. I hate to see my two fine caballeros snarling at each other. There's enough ugliness outside without us bringing it into this house. This has always been a home of laughter, not of quarrelling. Just because the rest of world is going mad, let us not follow its example.'

(3)

The conversation at dinner that evening was subdued. Angelina had forbidden all further discussion about the attempted assassination of General Gomez or anything to do with the current political situation in the country. For his part, Luis was grateful to his wife but Ramón was moody, though because of his love for his mother, he too refrained from any mention of the topics she had declared taboo. But to him it seemed that his father was refusing to face up to the realities of the situation and his mother was not helping by collaborating in his self-deceit. He remembered María saying that these things needed to be discussed. Things were not going to change because one decided to try and ignore them. Perhaps his mother was right and it was the increasingly obvious brutality of the government that was worrying his father. Until recently his father had always championed the people, their freedom and the rule of law, arguing that the former was impossible without the latter. It had made him critical of the army and especially of the Brigadas Especiales, yet now when people were beginning to express very similar sentiments and the National Guard were behaving in ever more outrageous ways, his father seemed to want the people to just go peacefully back to work as if nothing had happened. Ramón could not understand why both his parents seemed suddenly to have retreated into a little world of their own.

(4)

Luis Rodrigo watched his wife as she finished undressing and began to brush her hair. Once again, as he had so often done in the past, he caught himself thinking how lucky he was to have married such a beautiful and intelligent woman. Where another human being would question, she would remain silent and when eventually in his own time he voiced his thoughts he would discover that she had anticipated them. He looked at the line of her shoulders and how her hair glistened against the olive brown of her skin. 'Would you like me to do that for you?' he asked.

She turned to look at him. 'Yes Luis, if you would like to.'

He took the brush from her. He was conscious of her watching him in the mirror as he began to brush her hair and remembered that when they had been younger he had often brushed it before they made love. Somehow over the years, with the familiarity of marriage, their making love had been pared down to an increasingly brief interlude that preceded sleep.

Before placing the brush down, he kissed her shoulder. She tilted her head back and sighed. Luis Rodrigo straightened and stood looking down at his wife. Their eyes met and she smiled up at him. Her slightly parted lips excited him. Taking her hand, he led her to the bed.

Luis realised that he must have fallen asleep when he felt Angelina move beside him. Propping himself up on one elbow he turned his head to look down at her and their eyes met. 'Thank you,' he whispered.

'No. Thank *you*, my lover,' she replied.

'I love you, Angelina. I have always loved you.'

'And I love you, Luis.'

He lay back, looking at the ceiling, thinking. At length Angelina said, 'Tell me.' Her voice was slightly husky but he realised she was wide awake.

'It's Ramón,' he said. 'I'm worried about him.' He stopped but Angelina said nothing. 'Haven't you noticed a difference in him lately?' he asked.

'Yes, something's happened,' she replied. 'At first I thought that perhaps he's met a girl and I was glad but it seems political somehow.'

'That's what I think too. I'm worried. He seemed really pleased that someone had tried to kill General Gomez.'

'Well is that so bad?' Luis turned his head to look at his wife. 'Well is it?' she asked. 'Come on Luis, you yourself said the man is a butcher; that the army is out of control and that the Brigadas Especiales, in particular, are destroying the very social fabric of this country. General Gomez is their commanding officer, they were his brain child.'

'True but one cannot just kill those whom we dislike. I must say, Angelina, I'm surprised to hear you say such a thing.'

'Are you? I don't think you should be,' she replied. 'I hate violence, you know that, but I too see what is happening to this country. I don't think it's Ramón that you're worried about. I think it's what's happening all around us that's worrying you. Unless something is done and very soon, this country is going to have a full-scale civil war, that is what you are afraid of, isn't it? I know that's what really frightens me.'

'It's a possibility certainly,' he said slowly, 'but killing Gomez isn't going to help anybody. The army will just crack down even harder. Before all this blew up there was a chance the government would allow the sugar cane workers to form a union, even though the rebels were recruiting in the countryside. It could have been the beginning of real social reform.'

'Perhaps that is what the government fears.'

'Perhaps it is but now there isn't a hope in hell that they will loosen up. There will just be more arrests, even more shootings in the streets and more disappearances. They will use this as an excuse to arrest hundreds of people. Once they have been arrested it will become virtually impossible to trace them let alone defend them in court. Ever since they declared a state of emergency it has become impossible to operate the legal processes of the law. The law is being by-passed, made irrelevant.'

'And that's it, isn't it? You've said it yourself. That is what's been troubling you ever since that stupid election.'

Luis Rodrigo looked at his wife. The night seemed to have become very still. 'You humble me, my dear,' he said. 'You are both wise and beautiful. How was I ever lucky enough to marry you?'

Angelina reached across and touched her husband's

cheek. 'Sometimes you say such silly things, my dear. You're a kind and thoughtful man. It's why I married you. I am not so beautiful anymore, though it is nice to hear you say that you still think me beautiful. As for being wise, much of what I know I have learnt from you. As for Ramón, he is young and the young are always impatient for change. But he's a good boy. No, he's a man. A young man who cares about what is right.' Taking his hand she raised it to her lips and kissed the ends of his fingers. 'He too has learned from you. It is largely because of you that he has become the man he is. I like what I see and I don't think it is just the biased love of a mother for her son. He *is* young and we mustn't forget that, but I don't think he's likely to run off and join the rebels.'

'One doesn't have to do that to fall foul of the army, my dear. Just saying the wrong thing or being in the wrong place at the wrong time, can be enough.' He lay looking out of the bedroom window at the stars.

'I think Ramón knows that,' Angelina replied, 'but we can talk to him and make sure,' but even as she said it, she thought of Ramón standing listening to the speaker on the steps of the National Theatre and the worm of fear entered her soul. 'Put your arms around me, Luis,' she whispered.

Luis Rodrigo pulled his wife close to him but, unknown to him, it was a long time before she slept.

(5)

On Sunday Ramón waited for María as arranged, outside the Church of our Lady of Mercy but she did not show up. After checking that she was not still inside the church, he joined the general drift towards the Plaza de los Astros.

During Friday night, despite the curfew, posters had again appeared on the walls of several public buildings calling on the people to show their continued rejection of the election result. On Saturday, soldiers were seen making people tear these posters down and that night the television news included a government announcement banning all meetings of more than four people but by Sunday morning the posters were back. Everyone just assumed, or chose to assume, that attending church was exempt from this declaration and now, compelled by curiosity, they drifted en masse towards the Plaza de los Astros. There was no shouting and there were no banners. The crowd just made its way there with no more thought than a river making its way to the sea. They would probably have just melted away at the first sign of the National Guard, but strangely the army was completely absent from the streets.

Ramón's search for María made him one of the last of the people making their way towards the square, so he was also one of the first to hear the rumble of the approaching trucks behind him. He stood looking in the direction of the sound and then as he glanced back towards the plaza, a movement caught his eye. A man was running along behind the parapet on the top of the Consolidated Mines building. He was running bent over as if trying to remain hidden. Then he disappeared from view. Though Ramón had only been able to see the man for a few seconds, he felt sure that he had been carrying a gun. He looked back in the direction of the Church of our Lady of Mercy. The first truck could now be seen turning into the Calle de San Juan.

Ramón walked briskly into a side street and began moving away from the square. He had not gone far when another truck approached him, heading towards the Plaza de los Astros. It was full of soldiers sitting in two lines facing outwards, who stared at him as the truck roared past. He stepped into a doorway and watched as it came to a halt just before the intersection. The soldiers jumped out and began to erect a barbed wire barricade across the road. It was no more than a few strands of wire strung between wooden trestles but it effectively blocked the street.

Looking round Ramón saw a fire escape leading from a door on the top floor of the building opposite. Cautiously he made his way towards it, all the while watching the soldiers at the end of the street. Once he reached the fire escape he was hidden from their view until he passed the third floor. Then he could see the barricade and even part of the plaza beyond though he thought it unlikely that he himself would be seen. It had been the movement of the man on the top of the Consolidated Mines building that had caught his eye. He would never have been seen if he had kept still.

Ramón settled down, his back to the wall. The soldiers had finished erecting their barricade and were standing beside the truck, smoking. A man who seemed to be in charge of them spoke to the driver of the truck, which began reversing back up the street towards where Ramón now sat watching. The same man, obviously an officer, now started ordering the soldiers along either side of the street. They moved slowly as if reluctant to obey, until suddenly he lashed out at the man nearest him with the riding crop he was carrying. It caught the man across the face and he dropped his rifle. As he bent down to pick it up Ramón could clearly see blood streaming down his face. The soldiers moved quickly now until they formed a narrowing corridor behind the barricade, a sort of corral. The man with the riding crop then stood alone in the middle of the road like the conductor of an orchestra, though with his back to them, surveying the scene. Seemingly satisfied, he began slowly to pace backwards and forwards across the street, slapping the side of his leather boots with the riding crop as he did so. The men under his command continued smoking and talking among themselves but Ramón noticed that none of them took their eyes off the prowling man.

Nothing happened for nearly half an hour until

suddenly the sound of gunfire broke the Sunday silence. It came from the direction of the Plaza de los Astros and was followed almost immediately by something that sounded like the screaming of wild animals caught in a fire. It flooded into the street in a great wall of sound, rising in pitch as it grew louder. It went on and on, as did the gunfire and suddenly Ramón saw people running into the street in which he now sat. Men, women and children, they ran heedless of those amongst them who fell, a great shoal of humanity carried as if by a wave towards the barricade that now blocked their path. Ramón watched in horror as, before they reached it, the man with the riding crop ordered his men to open fire.

Ramón closed his eyes but the screaming and the gunfire forced him to open them again and he watched in horror as unarmed men, women and children were cut down by a remorseless hail of automatic fire. Then as suddenly as it had begun it was over. The silence that followed was made deeper by the moaning of the wounded. Only four people had made it through the barricade. They lay face down in pools of blood. Beyond the barricade there were people lying heaped on top of one another and a few were actually hanging over the barricade like washing left out to dry. One of these, a man apparently still alive, was vomiting blood, while trying to free himself from the wire and as he fell back Ramón could see that the whole of his chest cavity had been ripped open presumably by the gunfire that had virtually severed his left arm. He lay on his back twitching and kicking until his body suddenly arched and with one terrible last convulsion he flipped over onto his side and lay still.

This was the first demonstration in the capital of General Gomez' policy of the iron fist. A policy designed to deter all opposition and thus prevent further bloodshed. It also marked the coming of the civil war to the capital, which all but tore the heart out of the country of poets and dreamers.

(6)

'Oh thank God, thank God.' For the first time that Ramón could remember, his mother appeared to be on the verge of hysteria. 'Luis,' she called, 'he's here, he's safe.' Then turning to Ramón his mother said, 'Where have you been? We've been out of our minds with worry.'

'I'm all right Mother. Don't fuss.'

'Don't fuss!' Angelina looked at her husband as he entered the room. 'Did you hear the boy?'

Luis Rodrigo said, 'Your mother and I were worried about you, Son. Apparently people ignored the ban on demonstrations and then attacked the army. There's been some sort of shoot out in the Plaza de Los Astros. You could hear it all across the city.' Luis Rodrigo walked over to his wife and put an arm around her shoulder. 'We were afraid you might have got caught up in it. Your mother was worried sick; we both were.' Something in Ramón's face must have betrayed him because both his parents spoke at once. 'What is it Ramón? What's the matter?' A muscle in the side of his face began to twitch. Despite his effort at self-control he felt tears welling up in his eyes. His mother stepped forward and took his hands in hers.

'Get the boy a drink, Luis.' Angelina's voice though concerned was calm again. Ramón was thankful that she had not put her arms around him as he struggled to regain his self-control.

His father returned carrying a small glass of brandy. 'Here, drink this.'

Ramón drank some, it burned in his throat and he coughed. Someone patted him on the back. 'I was there,' he said. His parents did not seem to understand. 'I was there,' he repeated, 'in the Plaza de los Astros. Well not actually in it but nearby. I saw what happened.'

He began to tell them what he had seen. He told them how the soldiers were ordered to shoot the wounded before loading them into the back of the truck. He told them about the child, seemingly unhurt, who was lying on the ground crying beside its dead mother and how the man with the riding crop had walked over to it and shot it in the head. But he did not tell them about everything he had seen, and catching the expression on his mother's face he realised that she knew this. However, it was his father who seemed most affected by what he heard. Even as he looked at him, Ramón could have sworn he saw him bend, as if beneath an invisible load. But the family of Luis Rodrigo had as yet been but singed by the flames of war.

(7)

That night, during the television news, General Gomez himself addressed the nation on behalf of the president. He said that despite the government's ban on demonstrations, a demonstration had nevertheless taken place earlier in the day. When the National Guard attempted to break this up, they had been fired upon by gunmen hidden in the crowd. The National Guard therefore had no choice but to return fire. Regrettably there had been many casualties. He hoped this would serve as a reminder to all, that the government would not tolerate civil disorder and that any such violation of the law would be met with the utmost severity.

He ended his address by saying that it was the duty of everyone to support the democratically elected government that had come under attack from traitors and bandits but that these self-styled revolutionaries were in fact no more than common criminals.

In the Rodrigo household it was Angelina who got up and switched the television off.

'Lies!' The rage that flooded through Ramón swept away the sense of grief that had preceded it. 'That was a pack of damn lies!' His mother saw and heard the anger in her son and was both relieved and sad at the same time but she said nothing.

'You can't know that son', his father said. 'You yourself said that you could only just see into the plaza. You don't know what happened there.'

'But I told you what I saw. The people I saw killed had no weapons. The officer shot a child in cold blood for God's sake!'

'I know son.'

'But?'

Luis Rodrigo remained silent. He did not doubt the truth of what his son had told them but Ramón seemed to think that the whole operation had been cynically planned. This he just could not accept. A poisonous silence seeped into the room. At length he said, 'I'm not justifying the behaviour of the army but the government has to maintain law and order.'

'Law and order!' Ramón sounded incredulous. 'You talk of law and order after what I have told you?'

This was too much for his father, he said, 'Yes. Yes I talk to you about law and order. Nothing that has happened today lessens the importance of the law, the opposite in fact.'

Ramón said, 'I'll tell you something else I saw.' From the bitterness in his voice both Luis and Angelina Rodrigo knew they were about to hear some new and terrible detail of the massacre.

'Stop!' Angelina's voice had a brittle edge to it. Startled, both Ramón and Luis stopped glaring at each other and turned to look at her. 'Please both of you,' she pleaded, 'can't you see what's happening to us? We all love the same things. We are not on opposing sides. We are a family. Don't let the poison of war, of hatred, into your hearts. Please both of you, listen to me, this doesn't help those who were killed.'

Silence again crept into the room but it skulked in the corners wary and unsure and fled as Ramón said, 'Let him talk about law and order to the relatives of those the army murdered!'

Luis Rodrigo turned on his heal and walked to the window and stood with his back to the room, looking into the garden.

Angelina said, 'Your father doesn't condone murder, you know that.'

'I know that,' replied Ramón, 'but he's not living in the real world. It's no longer just the Special Brigades or some other murder squad that's killing the people. Today the National Guard deliberately butchered totally innocent people. There is no law anymore. That is why there is no order.'

'And what do you propose?' asked his father, turning away from the window.

'I'm not proposing anything. I just can't stomach your talking about law and order when the army, that is meant to protect this country, is being used to terrorise it.'

'You're beginning to sound like one of the rebels.'

'Perhaps I am,' retorted Ramón.

Again Angelina said, 'Please, both of you, stop it. I can't bear to hear you talking to each other as if you are enemies.' But something inside her seemed to weaken as she saw the look that passed between her husband and her son.

Ignoring his wife, Luis Rodrigo said, 'And where will this country be if that motley band of Marxist lunatics manage to seize power?'

'Where is it now?' retorted Ramón.

'No society is perfect. All societies have a certain amount of injustice.'

'A certain amount of injustice!'

The scorn in Ramón's voice fuelled his father's desperation. He said, 'You sound as if you hold me personally responsible for what happened today.'

'Of course I don't but just how much injustice are you prepared to accept?'

'I've never accepted injustice,' replied his father. 'All my life I have worked both within and for the law.'

'It no longer exists!' Ramón was almost shouting. 'What you believe in has been swept away by events. Ordinary men, women and even children are being murdered on the streets and by the army that represents the state. A regime you still appear to believe in.'

'I have never defended murder. Often I have been critical of the behaviour of the National Guard.'

'That will be a comfort to those they killed today!'

'Ramón! I will not have you speaking to your father like that.' This time there was anger in Angelina's voice but before Ramón could reply, she turned to Luis saying, 'And you're not much better. You know the boy is upset. We all are. Something very terrible has happened today and all you two can do is fly at each other's throats. No wonder this country is tearing itself to pieces. Here, my two champions of the law can do no better than snarl at each other like two stray dogs from a shanty town.'

At dinner later that evening conversation was stilted. The heat had gone from the argument but Angelina Rodrigo was saddened to realise that the disagreement between her husband and her son was as deep as the beliefs they shared and she was dismayed to discover that it was precisely those beliefs that were ultimately responsible for the chasm now opening up between them. She understood her husband's hatred of violence, his fear of civil war, coupled with his conviction that the rebels would prove little better than the existing regime and that this placed him in the intolerable position of seeming to defend a government that constantly violated more or less everything he held dear. And she understood her son's total rejection of any such standpoint. He was not so much embracing the doctrine of the rebels, as rejecting the idea that a government that was involved in killing, such as he had seen, could have any defence either moral or pragmatic and with an aching heart she realised that what she was witnessing in her own home would be happening throughout the country.

CHAPTER FOUR

(1)

It was hot inside the cab of the old truck. The time passed slowly as they clattered along the pot-holed road to the capital. Behind them a huge cloud of dust hid the mountains. They had been travelling since just after dawn and María felt exhausted by the constant effort needed to brace her feet against the bulkhead of the truck; it was easier for Juan who had the steering wheel to hang on to. From time to time he looked across at her and grinned, he seemed completely without fear.

'Do they ever search the trucks?'

'What did you say?'

'I asked if they ever search the trucks,' she answered, shouting above the roar of the engine.

'Sometimes.'

'What will you do if they search us?' It was a stupid question and María felt ashamed for having asked it but Juan just grinned at her.

'Why should they want to look at the truck when they have you to look at?' he replied. Then seeing the expression on her face he added, 'Don't worry they won't mess with you. In the countryside maybe; it could be dangerous but the road block will be on the outskirts of the city.' He looked across at her again. She gave him the best smile she could manage. 'We'll be all right,' he said, 'you'll see.'

The road was becoming a little better but the sun was higher in the sky. After another hour Juan said, 'We'll stop soon. I will give the land some water,' he grinned. He seldom spoke without a smile playing at the corners of his mouth. 'We can rest for a while. As long as we arrive before the curfew, we'll be all right.' The truck began to slow. He worked down through the gears and pulled to the side of the road. After the constant roar of the engine the silence soothed their tiredness but the heat as they climbed out of the cab hit them like the blast from an open furnace.

Juan disappeared off behind the truck and María stood looking back at the mountains. She would like to have stayed. The mountains were cool and silent; they offered sanctuary and a sense of peace, however illusory. She dreaded what she would find in the city. News of the latest massacre had reached the village the following day and she was afraid that Ramón might have been killed. She remembered the first demonstration when the army had fired into the crowd. She remembered the feeling of blind panic as she ran down the Calle de San Juan and she remembered the man covered in blood, who had been running beside her. She knew he had fallen but she had kept running. She did not know whether he had died but she could not forgive herself for not having even tried to help him and last night she had dreamt of Ramón similarly wounded and of her running heedlessly on, leaving him behind to die. She knew he would have gone to the Plaza de Los Astros to look for her.

'What is it?' Juan had returned.

'What?'

'What's the matter? Are you still worried about the road block'?'

'No. Well yes a little. It's not that.'

'What then?'

She looked at him. His face showed his concern for her. 'I was supposed to meet a man last Sunday,' she said. 'He would have gone to the Plaza de los Astros to look for me.'

Juan remained silent for a few moments before saying, 'We do not have to stop here; we can go now.'

'No. You need to rest.'

'You need to know,' he said.

'Getting back an hour or two sooner will change nothing,' she replied.

He looked at her for a moment and then nodded. 'You're right of course. Whatever has happened; has happened. I'm sorry. I hope he got away. Many did,' he added.

Looking at him again, María saw a sad man who hid

his sadness behind a smile. The simple man who always grinned was still there but she was aware of a seriousness and strength in him that she had not seen before. His was a calmness, an acceptance born of knowledge rather than of ignorance.

Seeing it made her more resolute. 'Let's eat,' she said.

After they had eaten sitting side-by-side leaning against the front wheel of the truck Juan said, 'Getting men into the city is easy. Getting our weapons into the city is proving to be harder. The countryside is ours. The army can destroy a village but they cannot destroy every village. Now we will bring the revolution into the cities. After last Sunday there will be many more who will help us.'

'There will be many who will be afraid,' said María.

'Yes and there will be many who are informers too but every new enemy of the National Guard is a possible friend of the Front.'

'What made you join the Front?' she asked.

'What made you?' he asked.

'I asked first.'

'True.' He smiled at her but said nothing while he rolled himself a cigarette. Then looking out across the coastal plain he said, 'I was working cutting timber. There were a couple of men who were in touch with the rebels. We all knew who they were but I suppose someone must have informed on them. One day the army came. They killed one of them in front of us. It wasn't nice. The other one, they took away with them. They had only just left when we heard an explosion and a lot of gunfire. About half an hour later the man they had taken away returned with a group of rebels. They had killed all the National Guard except two. Just about all of us wanted the rebels to kill them as well but we were told that they would be going with them. We were then asked if any of us would like to join the Front? I said I would. Best thing I've ever done,' he grinned at her. 'And you?' he asked, turning from his contemplation of the view. From where they were sitting they could see the capital in the distance beyond the lake.

'Did you ever find out who the informant was?' María asked.

He turned and looked at her for several seconds before saying, 'Later I learned that the army had already known the names of the two men in our camp, so it was decided to make their actual whereabouts known to the army. It was all part of a plan to draw the National Guard into an ambush. Unfortunately they arrived before the ambush was set up properly, so the rebels had to wait until they left the camp but by then they'd already killed one of the two men. The other one was lucky to survive the ambush but El Tigre said that even if he were killed, it would be better than being taken back to the capital for questioning. So the ambush went ahead anyway.'

María remembered her encounter with El Tigre but said nothing. Instead she said, 'You asked me how I became involved with the rebels. Years ago the army killed my parents.' She noticed his glance, 'I was very young,' she added. Juan remained silent. 'I think,' she continued, 'that I decided to join after I saw one of the Brigadas Especiales shoot one of the market traders because he objected to them stealing some of his oranges. When he cursed them, we were all afraid for him. We thought they would beat him up but then a captain came over and told him to shut up. When the man spat on the ground the captain just drew his revolver and shot him.' María paused, 'It was so casual. I think I realised then that our lives mean nothing; we might as well be slaves. They use us as they choose and when they wish to, they just kill us. It didn't seem to me that we had much left to lose. The Front offered the possibility of freedom, so when I was asked if I would take a message for them, I said yes.'

'So here we are,' said Juan.

'So here we are,' she replied.

'And your man, is he with the Front?' He could see that the question had taken her by surprise. 'There was some talk that he is from a wealthy family.' He saw the anger flash in her eyes. 'No one said anything bad,' he added.

'Has someone been spying on me?'

'Not me,' he replied holding up his hands. 'I only know what I heard, but if you are taking messages, it is likely that someone shadowed you to make sure that *you* were not followed.'

'That doesn't explain how they know about Ramón,'

she retorted. 'That's his name by the way,' she added self-consciously.

Juan noticed her embarrassment and looked away. 'It's different in the cities,' he explained. 'You could be watched at other times too, to see if anyone suspicious has become interested in you. That's probably how the Front knows about your Ramón.' He watched her as she considered this. 'If you are taking messages for the Front,' he continued, 'there's a danger that you might unwittingly lead spies to us, to other members of the Front. In the cities it's one of the ways the government tries to find out who their enemies are. We all have to try to protect each other. It's how we protect ourselves.'

She gave him a weak smile. She has fire in her, Juan thought and she's in love with her young man. I hope he hasn't been killed. The thought caught him by surprise. He glanced at her.

María said, 'You're a kind man.' He realised she had been watching him; might even have guessed what he'd been thinking. She said, 'I'm sorry I got angry. I'm just worried, I suppose.'

'That's natural.' He smiled at her encouragingly and was glad to see her smile a real smile back at him.

'He's nice,' she continued, 'not like most of the rich. But he has only just begun to see what's really happening in this country. It's easier for the poor to understand but he cares and he begins to see.'

'You make him see?' asked Juan.

'Perhaps. I help.' She gave him a sly smile.

They lapsed into silence. After a while he said, 'Well, I suppose we ought to go.' He realised that both of them were reluctant to get moving. Before climbing back into the truck they both took a last look at the mountains.

(2)

As they approached the city they could see the roadblock ahead of them. 'Well, here we go,' said Juan. 'Stay in the cab unless they actually tell you to get out.'

There was an old red truck already at the roadblock that they had not seen on the road ahead of them. The National Guard were talking to the driver, an old man bent nearly double by some illness. As Juan got out of the cab the guards waved the old man away and began walking towards him. María pulled her dress down over her knees. Almost immediately one of the men said, 'Oh, a pretty girl. Look Pedro, a pretty girl has come to see us and in such a battered old truck too.' Then turning to Juan he said, 'This your woman?'

'Yes,' Juan lied.

'She's your wife then?'

'No, we are not yet married.'

'Then she's not really your woman, is she?' said the guard called Pedro. Juan said nothing.

'Come down out of there, pretty one. Let us have a look at you.'

'Leave her alone,' said Juan.

'Did you hear that, Pedro? The man told me to leave the pretty girl alone.' The first guard turned back towards Juan. There was malice in his eyes. 'You,' he said walking up to Juan, 'need to learn to have some respect.' He stood in front of Juan, looking him up and down. 'What do you need to learn?' Juan remained silent. 'I asked you a question, dog breath!'

'I need to learn to have some respect,' replied Juan.

The National Guardsman stood looking at him. Juan could feel his disappointment. 'Yes, that is what you need to learn,' the man said slowly before turning away.

Suddenly they all became aware of the old man's truck. Its engine was refusing to start. The engine coughed but would not fire. The guard shouted, 'Get that heap of shit out of here!'

The engine kept spluttering but refused to start. The driver gave an exaggerated shrug of his shoulders, 'It's an old vehicle,' he said.

'You,' screamed the guard, turning back to Juan, 'Get that heap of junk out of here. Be gone from my sight, all of you!'

Juan walked to the door of the old man's truck. 'We'll push you down the road a bit. I'll have a look at the engine then, when we're away from those sacks of shit,' he said, nodding his head in the direction of the two National Guardsmen.

The old man grinned. 'Gracias, Señor. Perhaps the

engine will start after a bit of a push.' Juan noticed a gleam in the old man's eyes, as he turned back to his own vehicle.

'What are you waiting for? Vamos! Go, be gone from here!'

The soldier suddenly fired off a couple of rounds into the air. Juan jumped up into the cab and started the engine. 'You all right?' he asked.

'Of course but please, let's get out of here before that madman shoots somebody.'

Juan edged his truck in behind the other until they felt a slight bump and then as they began to move forward he brought in more power. The two vehicles moved off towards the city. In his mirror Juan could see the two National Guardsmen returning to their hut beside the road. Just then the truck in front of them began to pull away. The driver gave them a couple of blasts of his horn and a wave of his arm and the two vehicles began moving independently along the Avenida de Patriotismo and on in towards the centre of the city.

'Thanks for what you did back there, but you should be more careful,' María said.

'You have nothing to thank me for,' replied Juan. 'If I hadn't said something, he might have become suspicious and searched the truck. He just wanted an excuse to bully somebody. They wouldn't really have bothered you, not here. I told you, it's too near the city.'

'I was frightened just the same,' she replied.

'If they'd found the weapons then we would both have had something to be frightened about,' he said. 'I didn't like the idea of your riding with me, but apparently El Tigre gave specific orders that you were to ride back in the truck. He said a pretty woman would distract the attention of the soldiers.' Suddenly he began to laugh. 'It didn't take you long to do that.'

'Oh thanks,' she replied but María was laughing too as the old truck ahead of them swung off right down a side road. The driver gave them one last wave as they went their separate ways and Juan gave him a blast from the horn. It sounded more like a wail of protest. 'It's an old vehicle,' he mimicked the old man, with an exaggerated shrug of his shoulders and they both laughed until the tears rolled down their cheeks.

(3)

The men nodded to each other as they entered the room. Those that knew one another exchanged brief greetings but conversation was guarded and conducted in little above a whisper. Suddenly, a man in military uniform entered, followed by two men carrying weapons. The man in the uniform walked to the table at the front of the room and turned to face the men assembled before him. Without any preamble he said, 'I am known to some of you as El Tigre.' A murmur passed briefly through the gathering. When it had subsided he said,

'Since we decided to bring the revolution to the city, we have lost five comrades; five brave men.' He paused; there was complete silence in the room. 'We were unlucky not to kill Gomez but we have killed eighteen of the enemy. Five of us, for eighteen of them.'

What sounded like a low growl of approval went up from those present. Pablo Herendez raised his hand for silence. 'Of far greater importance however, is that we have made a good showing. Partly as a result of this and partly thanks to General Gomez, we have made many new friends. The city is no longer a hostile environment for us. We're seen for what we are; friends of the people and increasingly they'll help us as we demonstrate that we can strike at the very heart of this filthy and corrupt regime.'

A small but uncertain cheer sounded in the room. El Tigre waited until this had subsided. 'Some of you,' he continued, 'lost loved ones in the latest atrocity committed against unarmed people in the Plaza de los Astros. Again he paused as the mood in the room changed. 'Do not think that the killing of eighteen of those responsible is the end of the matter. We have only just begun. We now have effective control of the countryside. At night the roads are ours. The National Guard cower in their camps. Now we will kill them in the streets of the cities. We will kill them at their roadblocks. We will kill them whenever we see an opportunity to do so. The earth will turn red with their blood.' With sudden fury El Tigre brought his fist crashing down onto the table. 'Now we will hunt them!'

A howl of approval erupted into the silence. When this had subsided Pablo Herendez proceeded to outline his strategy for the battle of the cities.

In the three years it took the rebels to bring the regime to its knees and finally oust the president, many thousands died, many were maimed and many hearts were irreparably broken but as both General Gomez and El Tigre would have said, *'war is serious business and one cannot make an omelette without breaking eggs'*.

(4)

Manolita Hortez was scared. She had learned not to think of the other wives whose husbands would not be coming home again. It was her way of coping with the ever-present fear that one day Miguel would go out of the door and never come home again. As he himself had said, *'Death goes with the territory'*. It was part of the job, and for her, part of being a soldier's wife. This she had learned to live with. She was even aware that in a strange and terrifying way it made their time together clearer, brought it into sharper focus, made it more intense. It was as if they were conscious of living in borrowed time. It made them gentle with one another, closer, but now she felt helpless.

Manolita knew that it was not fear that made Miguel

so quiet. He had spoken of a new savagery, a sort of madness that was spreading like plague through the country and it was because of this that he was so quiet. As a woman, she could understand this. It all seemed so inevitable and so desperately sad. Like her husband, Manolita even had some sympathy for the rebels. She and Miguel had discussed what she called politics but what he said was no more than social justice. In a country of staggering poverty and unimaginable wealth, she found comfort in the Catholic reassurance of a better life to come. Miguel on the other hand argued that religion should be about the here and now, about life and how it was lived. Once she had said, only half jokingly, that he should perhaps have joined the rebels rather than the National Guard. To which he had replied that perhaps she was right but that things had been very different when he had first joined the army. Then he had regarded himself as lucky to have been accepted into the National Guard. Even his parents had been proud. As a young man he had looked forward to things changing but not just for himself or even his family but for all ordinary people, like the people he grew up amongst. However, during the twenty years he had served the state he had seen the rich becoming richer, the poor becoming poorer and the government becoming ever more repressive. As a member of the National Guard he now found himself part of the instrument of that repression. Far from feeling proud he felt trapped, dirty and betrayed.

Things had come to head after the first massacre in the Plaza de los Astros. He and Manolita had talked things over and Miguel decided that the best thing to do was to talk to Colonel Escobar. This had proved to be a waste of time and if that was not bad enough, it had been followed almost immediately by the attack on General Gomez.

Manolita feared that her husband was near breaking point but it was hard to get him to talk about what he was feeling. All he had really said so far was that the news reports were nonsense. With an aching heart she waited for him to begin to talk about what was troubling him. Meanwhile Jaime awoke in the next room and started crying. To her surprise Miguel got up almost immediately and brought him back into their bedroom with him. Manolita watched as he tried unsuccessfully to comfort the child.

'Here give him to me.' It took her a few minutes to quieten Jaime during which time Miguel remained standing looking down at them both in a way that unnerved her but she said nothing.

When Jaime eventually stopped crying Miguel said, 'Forgive me.'

Manolita did not understand but she just said, 'There is nothing to forgive you for.'

'I wish to God that were true,' he replied. He looked searchingly at her, then said, 'The other day I saw a women with a child no older than Jaime shot by the army I am a part of.' He saw her eyes widen in disbelief.

'But why?'

Almost reluctantly he continued. 'It had all been decided beforehand. On the direct orders of General Gomez we were told to make sure there would never be another demonstration in the Plaza de los Astros. Members of the Brigadas Especiales were with us, they began the shooting. We were then given direct orders to open fire too'.

'What happened to the child?' Manolita asked in a strangled whisper.

'What?'

'The child; what happened to the child?' she repeated. 'Was it killed?' Miguel did not answer. He just stood there with his head bowed looking down at the floor. She got up and took Jaime back into the kitchen. When she returned, Miguel was sitting on the bed. She sat down beside him. 'Miguel' she said gently. She repeated his name when he did not look at her, 'Miguel you must talk to me. You cannot keep this inside you like a poison.' She touched his arm gently. 'Please Miguel; you must try.' He nodded but remained silent.

After a while she said, 'Were very many people killed?' She was amazed that she managed to ask the question without feeling anything. To her surprise he answered almost immediately.

'No. Many got away. Soon after the army opened fire we came under fire ourselves. There were rebel snipers on the roofs.' He gave her a thin smile. 'Up until then many of my men had been aiming to miss anyway, I'm sure of it but after we found ourselves being shot at we concentrated on the snipers. That's when a lot of the people got away.' He paused, 'There were only three of them but we had eighteen killed and another eleven wounded. They did well, those three,' he added.

'But the rest of the people in the square, they didn't have guns?'

'No.'

'And you were told to shoot them.'

'Yes,' he replied wearily.

'Madre de Dios, I don't believe it.'

'It's true.'

'Oh I know it's true. But why? Why murder totally innocent people?'

'I've already told you. The government don't want any more demonstrations,' he replied.

'So they just kill anyone…' Manolita shook her head in disbelief. 'What about the men?'

'What about them?'

'Will they just do everything they are told to do?'

Miguel Hortez looked at his wife. At length he said, 'You know what happens to soldiers who disobey orders Manolita.'

'But that's monstrous. Surely…'

'The Brigadas Especiales can kill whoever they please. That's how it works. If a soldier were to refuse to carry out an order he would be shot on the spot. It's kill or be killed.'

Manolita noted the despair in his voice. 'So the National Guard now kills women and children.' Miguel Hortez said nothing. Manolita had sounded like she was talking to herself anyway. After a long time she asked, 'What are we going to do Miguel?'

'What can we do?' he replied.

(5)

Angelina Rodrigo was thinking about how to bring about a reconciliation between her husband and their son when she became aware that the maid had entered the room. 'What is it Cinchona?' she asked.

'Please Señora, a young lady came to the door asking for Señor Ramón. When I told her he was not here, she asked to leave this.'

'A letter?'

'Yes Señora.'

'What sort of girl was she?' The maid looked uncomfortable. 'Well was she pretty?' Angelina asked with a smile.

'Oh yes, Señora, very pretty.'

'But?' Cinchona stood looking at the floor. 'But?' repeated Angelina gently.

'I think she's trouble, Señora.'

'Trouble?' Angelina repeated in astonishment. 'What do you mean?'

'Please, I'd rather not say Señora.'

Angelina wished to pursue the matter but looking at Cinchona there was no mistaking the distress the girl was in, so she merely said, 'You'd better give me the letter.'

'Will that be all, Señora ?'

Angelina looked at the envelope. There was no writing on it and it was both slightly crumpled and a little grubby. 'How old was this girl?' she asked.

'About the same age as the young master Señora, perhaps a little younger.'

Angelina looked enquiringly at the maid who somehow managed to avoid looking at her. 'You didn't like her?'

'I didn't say that, Señora.'

Angelina decided to try a different approach. 'Have you ever seen this girl before?' she asked.

'I really couldn't say Señora.'

'Surely,' Angelina said irritated, 'you know whether or not you've seen her before?' She watched Cinchona's face but the girl remained stubbornly silent. 'Very well Cinchona,' sighed Angelina, 'that will be all.'

'Thank you Señora.'

Thoughtfully Angelina watched her leave the room.

Back in the safety of the kitchen Cinchona wished she had said nothing of her fears to the Señora but the young woman who had come to the door spelled danger. Cinchona knew a político when she saw one. She wished she had waited and given the letter to Ramón personally;

she could speak more freely to him. Though she was seven years younger they had always got on well together. In the past he had treated her almost like a younger sister. More recently a certain formality had crept into their relationship but this was no more than the situation demanded and the Rodrigo family was a good family to work for even if the Señora had become more difficult to please of late. Cinchona was well aware of the recent tensions within the household. The Rodrigos had always been a happy family but the recent unrest seemed to spill over into the lives of everybody.

While Cinchona had little sympathy for the rebels, she knew what happened to people who came to the attention of the authorities. It only took an opinion rashly expressed for the Brigadas Especiales to come and take people away and usually those people were never seen again. Cinchona shuddered as she began to prepare the Señora's lunch.

(6)

Juan and Rafino lay on the roof of the warehouse and watched as the man walked slowly down the street. It was becoming unusual to see a member of the National Guard on his own in uniform, even in the daytime. This one was an officer too. With two hours to go before the curfew his body might not even be found before the morning. For the third time, Juan checked that the rifle was loaded. He was aware of Rafino watching him; Juan could almost feel the man's excitement. He looked back at the soldier and then at the rest of the street to make sure that the officer was not being shadowed by a patrol. He saw a mother grab her child by the arm and drag him after her. The little boy still had his head turned in the direction of the soldier. Juan saw the soldier smile at the child.

'Do it. Do it now,' Rafino hissed.

'Quiet!' Juan slid the weapon forward and sighted along the barrel, aiming at the man's chest. The sound of a truck approaching from the opposite direction floated clearly up from the street. Good, he thought the noise will help mask the sound of the shot. His finger began to tighten around the trigger but suddenly the man just disappeared. At almost the same moment he heard a woman scream, followed by the screech of brakes. Taking his finger from the trigger, Juan looked towards the sound. The truck had come to a stop more or less where the soldier had been. The soldier was lying beside the road, a child virtually under him. At first, Juan thought the truck had done his job for him but then he saw the man move. He was getting up, apparently with some difficulty. The mother and child were the same he had watched a few seconds earlier. The mother was now holding the little boy to her and speaking to the soldier. Juan could not hear what she was saying but it was obvious that she was thanking him for saving her child's life. A small crowd was beginning to form around them.

Beside him he heard Rafino say, 'Shoot. Why don't you shoot? Shoot, now, while he is standing still. You still have a clear shot.'

Juan pulled the rifle back towards him. 'Get down!' In his excitement Rafino had got up onto his knees. 'Get down, you son of a whore. Do you want everybody in the street to see you?' As if only now aware that he could be seen from below, Rafino looked down into the street and then slid down beside Juan again. 'No one saw me.'

'How in the name of the Virgin do you know that?' But even as he spoke, it occurred to Juan that Rafino might be mad. 'Oh never mind,' he added, 'but be quiet and for the love of God stay out of sight.'

Juan looked down into the street. No one was looking up in their direction but a small crowd was now gathered round the soldier and the woman with the child. The opportunity for a shot had passed. He was glad. To shoot the man now would be like repaying a good deed with a bad one, a kind of sacrilege.

As if sensing his thoughts, Rafino said, 'You're going to let him go aren't you?'

Juan looked at him and saw the hatred in his eyes. He said, 'There are people all around him. It's impossible.'

'Now maybe, but it wasn't before,' said Rafino. Juan said nothing. 'You spared him because he saved the child, didn't you?' The note of contempt in Rafino's voice was unmistakeable. It was an accusation not a question. Juan removed the bullet from the breech of the rifle. 'That man is a member of the National Guard,' Rafino continued, 'the enemy and you decided to throw the whole operation because for once in his miserable life he did something decent. He's still the enemy. You are playing at war!' Juan looked at him coldly. Rafino glared back. 'El Tigre will hear of this,' he snarled. Then hardly bothering to crouch he made his way toward the fire escape leading down from the roof. Juan watched him go with a mixture of anger and disgust before once again turning his attention to what was happening below.

Down on the street Captain Miguel Hortez waved the driver of the truck away. The man, who was clearly terrified, fled and stalled the engine of the truck before moving off. The young woman too seemed torn between genuine gratitude for what the soldier had done and other emotions Juan could only guess at.

For his part Miguel Hortez was also aware of the mixed emotions of the woman whose child he had saved. Sadly he reflected that the days when he could walk freely among the people were past but right now his immediate problem was walking at all. He realised that his leg was not broken though the whole of his body seemed bruised by the impact of the truck. He looked at the little boy who turned away, hiding his face behind his mother's dress. Probably in shock but physically unhurt, thought the captain as he smiled weakly at the child's mother.

As he limped painfully away, Miguel Hortez had the

uncomfortable feeling that he was being watched, and not just by the crowd still surrounding the woman and her little boy, but the feeling passed as he turned into the Calle de los Martires.

(7)

Traffic was light on the Avenida de Patriotismo as Colonel Escobar's Jeep approached the outskirts of the city. What there was pulled over as his vehicle came up behind them. He grimaced as his driver fluffed a completely unnecessary gear change. In the back, his personal assistant clung to the vehicle with grim determination.

As soon as the checkpoint came into view, it took Colonel Escobar less than a second to realise that something was wrong. 'Pull over and stop,' he ordered. His driver changed down, again crunching the gears as he did so. 'Now!' roared the colonel. 'Weapon,' he said turning to the man in the back who handed him an M16 rifle.

His frightened driver brought the Jeep to a shuddering stop. 'Cover me you two, and spread out.' Colonel Escobar was already running half crouched, towards the hut, the barrel of the M16 weaving from side to side as he ran.

The door of the hut was slightly open. From inside came the buzz of flies. The colonel swore quietly to himself. He looked for any signs of a booby trap and seeing none pushed the door with his foot. A sweet sickly smell wafted out of the darkness. He stepped inside. An angry black cloud of flies swarmed in the corner of the hut showing him where to look. The men lay with the curious inelegance of the dead. He saw that their throats had been cut. Then he noticed the message scrawled in blood on the wall, *'You next.'* Smiling grimly to himself he turned to leave. The silhouette of his driver filled the doorway. Wild rage flooded through him. He had told the men to cover him, not follow him but he just said, 'Nothing to be done here,' as he moved past the man and out into the fresh air. He was pleased to see that his personal assistant was covering their backs and guarding the Jeep. From behind him came the sound of his driver retching. He walked back to the vehicle.

CHAPTER FIVE

(1)

Turning to her husband Angelina asked, 'Shall I turn out the light?'

'Yes all right.' Luis and Angelina Rodrigo lay in bed beside each other, neither ready for sleep. After a while Luis said, 'It's odd how sometimes we seem to need the darkness before we can work out what it is we really think.'

'Like how you used to kiss me when we were courting, you mean?' Angelina said, in an attempt to lighten his mood.

'What do you mean?'

'You always closed your eyes when you kissed me,' she replied.

'Didn't you close yours?' he asked.

'Not always.'

Luis let his mind wonder briefly back over the years. Theirs had been a good marriage, he reflected. Returning to the present he said, 'Stupid question, I suppose.'

'Why stupid?' asked his wife.

'Because you must have had your eyes open to see that mine were closed,' he replied.

'Oh, you!'

'You advocate?' he prompted, smiling to himself.

'You swine,' she retorted.

They fell silent again. Angelina waited. From somewhere across the city came the wail of a siren drowning out the sound of the cicadas, shattering the illusion of peace. 'I don't see why they need to use those damn things when there's a curfew anyway,' muttered Luis. Slowly the sounds from the garden drifted back into the room. He said, 'You don't really think I'm a swine, do you?'

'What sort of a question is that? No, of course I don't think you're a swine. What's all this about, Luis?'

'I've been thinking about the other night.'

'Your row with Ramón?'

'Do you think he really despises me?'

'Of course he doesn't. You were both angry.' It's been preying on his mind ever since, she thought.

'He was very rude.'

'He was very upset,' she said gently.

'Yes, I suppose so.'

'You both were,' she added.

'Yes,' he said. Angelina waited. 'What I mean is,' he continued, 'do you think Ramón sees me as part of the horror just because I'm against the rebels? I'm only against them because the country would be bankrupt within six months if they were to come to power. Besides it presupposes a civil war that the rebels won. Imagine it. A civil war for God's sake! Once it really got going the country would be torn apart. Better the devil we know. If the people would just go back to work, things would quieten down; get better.'

'Do you really believe that, Luis?'

'Yes of course,' he said uncertainly. 'Don't you?'

'What about all the corruption,' she asked; 'all the abuses? You often complain that this government is riding roughshod over just about everything you believe in.'

'You're beginning to sound like Ramón.'

'I'm only reminding you of what you yourself often say. You're hardly an admirer of the president are you? As for what Ramón thinks, you must know that he believes in the same things you do.'

'Yes I suppose so, but don't you see, my dear, the fighting has to stop in order for the country to be able to get back to normal.'

'But that's what we're talking about, isn't it Luis? What has passed for normal for the last God knows how many years. Only things are getting worse, aren't they? You of all people know that.'

When Luis remained silent Angelina searched for his hand beneath the bed cover. 'Luis I know you love me and I love you but so too does Ramón,' she gave his hand a little squeeze.

'I know. I know my dear.' He turned and kissed her.

'We're probably all a little on edge,' she added. Outside in the garden the cicadas murmured their agreement.

After a while he said, 'I think it's the feeling of helplessness, as if we are all caught in the path of a hurricane. There's a horrible inevitability about it all and yet it's all so predictable.'

'Surely there's got to be an alternative?'

'You tell me,' he sighed. 'But you're right about things getting worse, though I can't see how having a civil war is going to make them any better.'

'Perhaps someone will kill the president or that monster Gomez.'

'Ah, the general again. I recall that both you and Ramón seemed disappointed when those two young men failed to kill him.'

'Only because as long as he is alive the army will continue to make a mockery of the rule of law you hold so dear.'

'You make it sound like an indulgence,' he protested.

'I didn't mean to.'

'The point is though, that what you seem to be suggesting is that the rule of law can best be served by breaking it.'

'Perhaps in special circumstances, it's the only way,' she replied.

'And who decides when the circumstances are special?'

'I don't know Luis, but how are things going to get better without the overthrow of this government?'

'If I knew that,' Luis Rodrigo began, but he left the sentence unfinished.

'And meanwhile?'

'Meanwhile how can you be so sure that killing General Gomez will bring about the changes you desire?'

'Well it certainly wouldn't do any harm.'

'Apart from the dubiousness of that proposition, what about its morality?' he asked.

'Words, Luis. Words. The man is a monster. The people the Brigadas Especiales kill are real people. Where is the morality in their deaths?'

'So one evil justifies another?'

'Of course not but you are assuming that to kill is necessarily evil. Gomez is a rabid dog, he needs to be destroyed.'

'Perhaps,' conceded Luis at last. They were both tired of arguing. The night embraced them. Angelina turned on her side and sliding her arm across her husband's chest kissed his ear. He turned towards her only half responsive but quickly she seduced him, drew him to her and as the curfew wore on towards the dawn, they fell asleep in each other's arms as they had so often done throughout their marriage, while outside the orange Jeeps of the Brigadas Especiales Contra Actos de Terrorismo continued to prowl the now silent streets of the capital.

(2)

'What's the matter?' Ramón asked with a smile. 'You look as if you've lied to the priest at confession.'

'Oh, Señor Ramón,' the maid looked genuinely alarmed, 'you should not speak that way, you will bring misfortune down upon yourself.'

'Calm yourself Cinchona, it was just a joke,' he said trying to reassure her.

She looked at him doubtfully. 'You are not cross with me?' she asked.

'Cross with you?' he repeated puzzled. 'Why would I be cross with you?'

'About the letter, I mean.'

'What letter?' he asked puzzled. Then seeing that this seemed to further distress the maid, he softened his voice and repeated, 'What letter are you talking about Cinchona?'

'You were not at home,' Cinchona began nervously, 'so I gave the Señorita's letter to the Señora.'

It took Ramón a few moments to grasp the significance of what Cinchona was saying. Then he said, 'When did the letter arrive? How did it arrive?' Still slightly confused he added, 'Did you see the Señorita? Was she all right?'

'The Señorita herself gave me the letter,' replied the maid, 'and yes, she was perfectly all right.'

Ramón gave a sigh of relief as Cinchona said, 'You have not received it?'

'You mean has my mother given me the letter? No she has not,' he said irritated. Then mistaking the cause of the worry he saw on the girl's face, he added, 'Don't worry Cinchona, you are not in trouble over this.'

'It's not the Señora I'm afraid of,' Cinchona replied.

'What do you mean?'

'Oh, Master Ramón, please be careful. She could bring trouble to all of us, that one.'

Ramón stared at her. 'What makes you say that?' he asked uneasily.

'Forgive me, Señor Ramón, if I have spoken out of turn.'

Ramón waited but Cinchona remained silent. He noted the way she managed to avoid looking at him. 'Look at me,' he said. Obediently she did so. 'It is I, Ramón,' he said gently, 'whom you have known since you entered service. We are friends, are we not?' He smiled encouragingly at her. The girl nodded but he noticed that she remained ill at ease. Disappointed he said, 'So I ask you again, what makes you think that the Señorita, she's called María by the way; what makes you think she could possibly be a danger to any of us?' Cinchona looked searchingly into his face. He noticed that her eyes seemed unnaturally wide.

'She speaks to dangerous people,' the maid replied. 'I have seen her in the market and the soldiers notice a beautiful woman. They will have noticed her. They will remember. If they arrest her they will become interested in all who know her.'

Ramón looked thoughtfully at the girl. 'Do you like her?' he asked.

'She is very beautiful.'

'That is not what I asked you,' said Ramón with a smile.

'I do not dislike her as a person but she is a danger to all of us. She is not a good person to know.'

'But you do not like the soldiers?' He was sorry the moment he had asked the question. He thought Cinchona might actually turn and run from him but though she remained looking at him she was now clearly very frightened. 'I'm sorry,' he said. 'Don't be afraid. What I mean is,' he paused wondering what he did actually mean. He said, 'María is a good and kind person as well as a beautiful one.'

'Oh, I was afraid of this,' wailed the maid. Before he could recover from his surprise, she said, 'You're in love with her aren't you?'

He looked at her in astonishment. 'This conversation is most improper,' he began but then with a grin added, 'Yes; yes I am.' Then serious again he said, 'Nothing is going to happen to María.' The maid looked as if she were about to reply but thought better of it. 'What were you going to say?' he invited her.

'If you are not afraid for yourself,' blurted out the girl, 'what about your parents?' She was almost in tears. 'If the army were to come to this house,' she continued in a voice which seemed to quiver, 'what do you think would happen to me?'

'Cinchona please, nothing is going to happen to you or to my parents.'

'Oh, Master Ramón, how can you say that? You know what is happening. Everyone is scared of the army or if they aren't, they should be. Even the Señora's position, your father's position, would not save them or the rest of us. If the army thought anyone in this house had anything to do with the rebels,' Cinchona gave a sob, 'they would kill us, all of us.' She began to cry.

Suddenly the girl's distress reminded him of how the National Guard had shot the wounded before throwing them into the back of the truck and he too felt afraid. In a dry voice he said, 'Cinchona I'm sorry. I didn't realise that you knew about such things but both María and I know too.' The girl sniffed and looked up at him. 'Of course I do not want anything to happen to her or to you or to my parents but what can I do? What can any of us do, except be as careful as we can?'

(3)

'We need to talk about this,' Angelina said as she gave Ramón the letter. 'Apart from anything else your lady friend has frightened Cinchona.'

'I know.'

'Your father must not know about this, not yet at least. That is why I didn't give you this before.'

Ramón said, 'He'll have to know sometime.'

Angelina looked searchingly at her son before saying, 'Ramón I do not wish to pry into your private life but you above all people must realise that in these times we all have to be careful whom we associate with, however innocently.'

'I do know that Mother.'

'Do you Ramón? Do you really?'

'It was me who told you and Father what really happened in the Plaza de los Astros remember?' replied Ramón. 'I know, as do my friends at the university, what the army is capable of. Years ago, long before I met María, that's her name by the way, the army killed her parents. We both know how dangerous the National Guard can be and I would never knowingly do anything to place you or Father, or Cinchona for that matter, in any danger.'

'I know that my son but your María may already have placed us in danger. Cinchona is terrified. She has seen her talking to people she thinks are rebel sympathisers. For all we know others may have noticed too and Cinchona may in the future even be forced to become a government informer, however long she has lived with us.'

'That could happen to anyone.'

'That's my point,' replied his mother. Ramón said nothing. Mother and son looked at each other. 'Is she very beautiful?' Angelina asked with a smile.

'I think so,' Ramón replied.

'So this is serious?'

'I suppose so. Well yes. Yes, it is.'

'So my son is in love.' Angelina smiled at her son.

'Mother!'

'Do not mind your mother. Your father and I are still in love after all these years. You are the fruit of that love. Both of us are proud of you but you are young and eager for change and God knows this country needs to change but please my son be careful and tell your María to be careful too. It would break my heart and your father's too, if something were to happen to you. Remember that and be careful for us as well as for yourself, my son.'

(4)

María's letter was just a note apologising for not meeting him as arranged and saying that she would be at the eight o'clock mass in the church of Our Lady of Mercy on Sunday morning. It was a curiously impersonal note that left Ramón disappointed and worried but he consoled himself with the thought that she had bothered to deliver it at all. He wondered how she had known where he lived and if she had been seen giving her letter to Cinchona. He now realised there were no second chances with either the Brigadas Especiales or the National Guard; both of whom now killed on a mere whim. He and María would have to be more careful in the future.

However, at eleven o'clock on Friday morning while

reading in the university library, Ramón became aware of shouting that was quickly followed by the sound of gunfire coming from just outside the building. He went to a window and saw soldiers running towards the library. He noticed that some had bayonets fixed to their guns. Other students were crowding in behind him. He moved away from the window, back towards the desk where he had been reading, still not sure what he was going to do when suddenly the window he had been looking out of shattered. Startled he turned to see one of the students who had been standing behind him stagger back into the room blood streaming down his face. 'My eyes, my eyes!' he screamed. 'I can't see. I can't see.'

Ramón watched as two of his friends led him, sobbing, back towards the reading desks, where they began to wipe away the blood with a handkerchief. 'I can't see, I'm blind,' he sobbed. Then Ramón heard more gunfire and shouting but coming from somewhere within the building itself. He ran to the library door and out into the hall. Looking down the stairwell he saw a soldier mounting the stairs. The man looked up and immediately raised his gun. Ramón stepped back as a short burst of automatic fire peppered the ceiling above him. He turned and ran down the hall, past the library door. He heard more gunfire and screaming behind him.

He paused to look back then turning he continued down the corridor and through a door marked Staff

Only. He tried the first door on the left but it was locked. He moved on, looking for a service stairway or lift to the ground floor. He tried two more doors, the first led to a storeroom full of cleaning equipment, the second to a small staff canteen. He turned a corner and came to a pair of double doors with glass in them and found that they led to a staircase. He began heading towards the stairs but stopped as he heard what sounded like a door being kicked open and smashing against a wall and then a man's voice shouting, 'Here's one,' followed by a single gunshot. He backed away, turned and went back into the hall. Almost immediately he heard more screaming and a prolonged burst of gunfire from the direction of the library. In desperation, he tried the door nearest him but it was locked. He heard a series of single gunshots coming from the library followed by silence. He opened the door to the little storeroom. Seeing a pair of overalls he grabbed them and hurriedly put them on. Then he picked up a mop and a bucket and looked out into the corridor. No one was in sight. Cautiously he made his way back to the staff canteen. A few moments later he heard the National Guard approaching. Then the door burst open and a soldier stepped into the room. 'Who are you? What are you doing here?' the man demanded. His gun was pointing straight at Ramón's chest.

'I heard all the shooting. I didn't want to get involved in any trouble,' Ramón replied.

The soldier moved further into the room. Another

soldier stepped into the room behind him. 'He's a student', the second man said, 'Shoot him!'

'No. I just work here,' protested Ramón.

For a moment the two men just looked at him. Then the soldier who had come into the room first said, 'We'll take him with us. They'll find out soon enough.' Looking at Ramón he said, 'You'd better not be lying to us.'

The two men followed him back along the corridor. The library doors were closed. Ahead of them a group of soldiers were making their way down the main stairs. The last one of them turned and looked back up at him. He looked familiar. His shirt was stained with sweat and he was overweight, his belly bulging out over his belt. Ramón realised that he was the same man who had fired at him earlier.

'Move!' He felt the barrel of a gun jab him in the back. He stumbled down the first three steps. The man in front of him must have failed to recognise him and was again just walking ahead of him down the stairs.

As they came out of the building, Ramón saw other soldiers coming out of other doors that opened onto the quadrangle that led directly to the main entrance of the University, now blocked by an army truck that was backed up to the open main gates. Ramón looked around him. He saw that one group of soldiers had two prisoners, both young women whom they told to kneel. Ramón was ordered to join them. One of them was a girl he had noticed while attending a lecture on jurisprudence. She recognised him and looked about to speak but Ramón shook his head at her slightly. She looked away at the soldiers standing around them. The young woman beside her said, 'What do you think they are going to do with us?'

'Silence! Prisoners are not permitted to speak to one another.'

Ramón turned towards the speaker. The man's face was an icon of absolute cruelty, a human face devoid of all pity and all humanity. He was standing, legs wide apart and he was looking straight at Ramón while gently slapping the side of one of his gleaming leather boots with a riding crop. Ramón was reminded of the flickering tongue of a venomous snake, as it tastes the air for the scent of its prey and he felt his whole body begin to tremble uncontrollably.

(5)

When Miguel Hortez entered Colonel Escobar's office the colonel was standing staring out of the window. 'Close the door Captain.' Miguel Hortez did so. The colonel remained with his back to Miguel Hortez looking out of the window. Miguel stood watching him. It was as if stillness emanated from the man. The ticking of the wall clock served only to emphasise his stillness and the silence in the room. Then without looking at Miguel Hortez, Colonel Escobar went and sat down behind his desk.

When he looked up, Miguel Hortez saluted. 'At ease, Captain.' Colonel Escobar looked steadily at him. Miguel Hortez returned his gaze. At length Colonel Escobar said, 'I have read your report,' he paused. 'In it you say that although the army met no resistance when it entered the university we nevertheless sustained two casualties. Is that correct?'

'Two of our men were killed, yes, Sir.'

'And yet neither you nor any of your men encountered any resistance whatsoever while you were in the university?'

'No, Sir. None of the students or staff appeared to be armed. In fact we found no weapons on the campus other than those belonging to our own two casualties.'

'And you do not actually know how, when or where these two men were killed?'

'Well no, Sir, but as I stated in my report, Sergeant Becerra and I found their bodies in the library though long after all the shooting was over and the Brigadas Especiales had driven away with the prisoners but we are fairly sure they died there and that they had both been shot at close range. In fact we definitely know one of them was because he had been shot in the head and there were powder burns on his face around the entry point. The other man had been shot twice, in the chest and also through the head. I believe they were both executed, Sir.'

'But we have no witnesses to this execution, if that is what it was?'

'No, Sir. When we got there everyone in the library was dead. In all there were twenty-seven bodies, including our two men. We believe the rest were all students. Most looked as if they had been killed by automatic fire though several had head wounds similar to our men. Four were females and all were lying on the far side of the room, as far away as they could be from the library door. Our men however, were both found just inside the library doors.'

The colonel rose from behind his desk. 'You may sit down Captain.'

'I prefer to remain standing, Sir.'

'What? Oh, as you wish,' muttered the colonel as he walked back to the window where he once again stood with his back to Miguel Hortez. Still looking out of the window he asked, 'Were there any other casualties among government forces?'

'Do you mean among the Brigadas Especiales, Sir?'

'Yes, among the Brigadas Especiales.'

'Not that I am aware of, Sir. No.'

'Is it possible, in your opinion Captain, that our men were killed by students or rebel sympathisers?'

'I think it most unlikely, Sir.'

'By fellow members of the National Guard then?'

'Not in my unit, Sir. Absolutely not.'

Colonel Escobar turned to face him. 'So what you are suggesting is that the Brigadas Especiales are responsible for the deaths of two of our men.'

'I really couldn't say, Sir.'

'Your report seems to leave little room for doubt Captain.'

'I have merely recorded what Sergeant Becerra and I found, Sir,' replied Miguel Hortez.

'Which strongly suggests that the Brigadas Especiales were responsible.'

Miguel Hortez remained silent. The two men looked at each other. At length Colonel Escobar said, 'Leave this with me Captain. Meantime you are not to discuss this with anyone. Is that understood?'

'Yes, Sir.'

'And I will want to know if this is being talked about among your men.'

'They are bound to talk about it, Colonel.'

'You are to forbid any such talk.'

'With respect, Sir, that will only fuel any suspicion the men may have about the circumstances of their deaths.' Miguel Hortez noticed Colonel Escobar's body tense. 'Besides Private Fernandez was a popular soldier, a brave and reliable man,' he continued, 'and a serious loss to our unit. They are bound to talk about his death. If I were to start trying to silence my men I would destroy their trust in me.' Miguel Hortez noticed Colonel Escobar's body relax. The fleeting impression of a crouching jaguar had passed.

'You are right of course.' Something between a snarl and a smile briefly contorted Colonel Escobar's face. The clock ticked. He sat very still staring down at the report on his desk. Miguel Hortez waited. At length Colonel Escobar said, 'Leave this with me, Hortez. Dismiss.'

'Thank you, Sir.' He left the room closing the door quietly behind him. He was aware of Colonel Escobar's personal assistant watching his every step as he walked out through the outer office. He suspected the man had been listening outside Colonel Escobar's door.

(6)

As the evening wore on tension within the Rodrigo household mounted. Since the early afternoon all scheduled broadcasts had been replaced by martial music until during a truncated news broadcast, General Gomez had once again addressed the nation saying that because the capital's university had become a hotbed of anti-government agitation, the National Guard, together with elite troops from the Brigadas Especiales, had, following direct orders from the president, entered the university campus in search of rebels and their sympathisers. Regretfully there had been some loss of life. As a result, the university would remain closed until further notice. He ended his statement with a reminder that it was the duty of all patriotic citizens to support the democratically elected government of the country.

Angelina Rodrigo switched off the radio. 'What are we going to do, Luis? Ramón should have been home long ago.' Luis Rodrigo saw his own fear reflected in his wife's face. Stepping forward he put his arms around her but after only a moment she pulled away from him. 'You're trembling,' she said accusingly.

'Am I? I'm sorry my dear.' He was disgusted by his own weakness.

'You're afraid something has happened to him aren't you?' He felt like an animal trapped in the headlights of a car. 'You are aren't you?'

'Angelina please.'

'Angelina please,' she mimicked. 'Angelina please! Do something. For God's sake Luis, do something.' Then suddenly, as if becoming aware of his pain, she stepped forward burying her face against his chest. 'I'm sorry Luis. I'm sorry.'

'I know.' He ran his fingers through her hair. 'I know. It's all right.'

'We've got to do something,' she sobbed.

Despite himself he felt tears welling up in his eyes. He kissed her forehead. Trying desperately to keep his own emotions under control he said, 'We can't do anything tonight.'

'He could be hurt.'

'He's probably hiding out with friends,' he said. 'Anyway where would we begin to look? Besides there's the curfew,' he added. 'We would probably just get ourselves shot.' He regretted it the moment the words had left his lips.

'Do you think that's what has happened to Ramón?' She looked imploringly into his face.

'I don't know, Angelina,' he answered truthfully.

'Oh, Luis, I'm so afraid.'

He was aware of his own fear as it stalked his remaining courage. 'I know,' he replied.

'He was supposed to be in the university,' Angelina reminded him unnecessarily. 'He could have been there when the army entered it and there was so much shooting.'

'Even if he was, he didn't have a gun. There would have been no reason for the army to shoot him.'

'Do they need a reason?'

He chose to ignore the question. Instead he said, 'On the news they said the Brigadas Especiales took a lot of prisoners.'

'That could be even worse.'

'Angelina stop it. This doesn't help Ramón or us. Tomorrow after the curfew is lifted, if he hasn't come home we will try and find out where he is.'

That night Luis and Angelina Rodrigo, like countless others before them, began their slow descent into hell.

(7)

In the morning they drove towards the eastern sector of the capital where the Brigadas Especiales had their headquarters. It was in the part of the city that had been particularly badly hit by the earthquake but, unlike the business district and immediate surroundings of the Plaza de los Astros where the majority of the foreign aid had been spent to showcase the nation's recovery, here the poverty of the shanty town that had sprung up after it, existed as a grotesque testament to the government's failure to address the plight of those worst affected by the disaster. What remained of the once elegant residential quarter lay like the carcass of a partially dismembered animal surrounded by the bustling chaos of a fetid slum.

They soon came to a roadblock manned by National Guardsmen. Luis slowed the car to a stop. One of the soldiers approached the car.

'No cars are allowed beyond this point,' the man said peering into the back of the car.

Luis said, 'We need to speak to an officer of the Brigadas Especiales.'

'And what business do you have with the Brigadas Especiales?' the soldier asked coldly.

'We wish to make enquiries into the possible whereabouts of our son,' Luis replied.

'And what makes you think the Brigadas Especiales would know anything about the whereabouts of your son?' The man's tone was contemptuous.

'He's a student at the university and he failed to return home last night. We understand from the news broadcasts that anyone detained by the authorities will be held by the Brigadas Especiales.'

'So he's a político,' the man sneered. 'Have you tried the city morgue?'

'No, he's just a student,' Angelina said, leaning across her husband. 'He does not concern himself with politics.'

'So what does this son of yours study?' the soldier asked, bending down to look across at Angelina.

'The law,' replied Luis.

'I didn't ask you,' the soldier snapped.

Before Luis could reply Angelina said, 'Please, we are just trying to find our son. We need to speak to someone who might know where he is.'

The soldier straightened up and looked hard at Luis before saying, 'Leave your car over there. After you have been through the barrier walk to the end of the block, turn left and the headquarters of the Brigadas Especiales is on the right. You will know it when you see it,' he added as he turned and walked back to rejoin the group of soldiers who were watching them with bored indifference.

Having parked the car Luis and Angelina again approached the barrier. The same soldier came forward to meet them.

'Raise your arms,' he ordered Luis. Luis Rodrigo did as he was told and the man patted him down. 'Now you.' Angelina raised her arms. The man brazenly groped her breasts before running his hands over her body and between her thighs. Angelina kept her eyes fixed on her husband's face, which had gone pale. The other soldiers looked on in anticipation, waiting for something to happen.

The soldier stepped back and turning to Luis said, 'Now Señor, you may proceed.' With exaggerated courtesy he raised the barrier for them.

Angelina grasped her husband's hand as they walked through to the street beyond.

'That bastard!' spluttered Luis in impotent fury.

'Luis!' Angelina hissed. He turned towards her, his face flushed with anger and shame. 'It doesn't matter.' She squeezed his hand hard. 'Luis, look at me.' When their eyes met she repeated, 'It doesn't matter. It is not important. We are here to try and find Ramón. For God's sake, Luis don't give them an excuse to kill you. What do you think would happen to me then? And anyway what could you possibly have done? Now forget it. Luis, please, for me.'

He nodded and looked away. 'Yes all right. All right,' he muttered.

Letting go of his hand Angelina said, 'At least we now know what we are walking into. We have to find out if they are holding Ramón and if we can do anything to bring about his release. Then we have to get back out of here alive. We won't do that if you allow them to provoke you.' She knew instinctively that she had touched a raw nerve. 'Luis I love you, please, I need a live husband not a dead hero. Don't get yourself killed. Don't leave me.'

He glanced across at her. Again their eyes met. 'All right,' he said again. 'All right, Angelina, but one day. One day!' he muttered savagely.

They walked on in silence. The street was eerily quiet. There were people about but without exception they all kept their eyes downcast or actually looked away as if determined not to notice them. Then, at the end of the street, just as they turned left they heard a terrible high-pitched scream. It was impossible to know if it had been made by a man or a woman and it lasted no more than a second or two but it was unmistakably the final agonised death shriek of a human being. Luis and Angelina looked at one another. Without even realising it, both of them had come to an abrupt standstill. The colour had all but drained from their faces as they stared in disbelief at one another.

'Madre de Dios,' whispered Angelina.

Reluctantly they walked on towards the building from which the scream had come. As they approached it, two men came out and climbed into one of the orange Jeeps that were parked outside. A third soldier came running down the steps after them and half jumped, half fell into the back of the Jeep. All three men laughed as the vehicle jerked forward. They were still laughing as it passed them and Angelina and Luis realised that all three men, including the driver, were drunk. They watched it turn left, its wheels spinning as it headed off towards the barrier. Then it was gone and, as the roar of its engine died away and the dust began to settle, the poisoned silence seeped back into the now empty street.

Slowly they climbed the steps, past the sign which read 'Welcome to the House of Dreams' and through the open door into what had once been a grand entrance hall. Now, however, a desk with a red telephone on it stood incongruously in the centre of the hall behind which a soldier sat slouched in a leather swivel chair with his feet up on the desk.

'Yes?' he said, as they approached.

Luis said, 'We wish to enquire into the possible whereabouts of our son.'

Lazily the man swung his feet off the desk and swivelling in his chair looked around the hallway. 'I do not see him here,' he replied.

Keeping his voice firm Luis said, 'I wish to speak to the officer in charge here.'

The soldier looked at him in surprise before a thin smile appeared at the corners of his mouth. 'I think we might be able to arrange that,' he said, picking up the phone. 'He's a busy man but I think perhaps he will find the time to speak to you. Who shall I say wishes to see him?'

'My name is Luis Rodrigo and this is my wife,' Luis replied.

The soldier dialled a two-digit number and waited. Somewhere on the floor above a phone rang. The sound barely breached the malignant silence in the hall before the ringing stopped and a distorted metallic sound came down the line.

'A Señor Rodrigo and his wife are here and wish to speak to you, Captain,' the soldier said looking up at them as he spoke. A garbled sound came out of the telephone. 'About their son.' The receiver crackled back. 'Yes, sir.' It crackled again and went dead. He replaced the receiver and got to his feet. 'Follow me.' He led them towards a sweeping curved staircase that led to the floors above.

CHAPTER SIX

(1)

It was as a result of the attack on General Gomez and the beginning of rebel activity within the city and surrounding countryside, that Colonel Escobar decided to double both the number of troops manning checkpoints and the escort that Three Brigade provided for the wages truck that once a month made its way from the capital to Sierra Plata, the small town that took its name from the silver mines nearby. However, it was this truck and its escort that were attacked just three days after his discovery of the two dead soldiers at the checkpoint on the outskirts of the city.

Both Juan and Rafino were among the twenty-six members of the Liberation Front that lay in wait for the little convoy as it came into view at the far end of the valley, a place known locally as the Valley of Ghosts because of the tribe of monkeys that inhabited it.

Both the Jeep and the wages truck passed the place where the explosives were hidden. Together with the other members of the Front, Juan watched as the truck full of soldiers approached the spot. There was a loud thud and the truck bucked like an unbroken stallion, throwing two of its occupants out of the back. Then it swerved off the road and with what sounded like a dry cough, the fuel tank exploded and the truck together with the remaining soldiers still in it, was engulfed in a ball of flame. Neither the screaming nor the gunfire lasted long. It was followed by a short period of silence as the dust settled and all eyes turned towards the wages truck and the Jeep, both of which had stopped.

Then a National Guardsmen who had been lying in the road got to his feet and made a run for it. At first he ran back along the road in the direction the little convoy had come from, in full view of everyone watching but suddenly he must have realised this because he swerved and started running towards the trees. Until that moment it was almost as if everyone was waiting to see how far he would get but a second or two later he was cut down by a hail of fire from at least half of those who had until that moment watched with a mixture of curious fascination and disbelief.

This was the cue for the Jeep to move. It lurched forward its wheels spinning, a cloud of dust rising behind it. It travelled approximately seven hundred and fifty metres before being fired upon by those who had patiently awaited its coming. Its occupants were all dead before it came to a standstill by the side of the road.

Then all the monkeys and birds, who until that

moment had seemingly been stunned into silence by the sound of the slaughter, began to howl and screech in what was in effect a strange and savage requiem for the fallen, as one by one the rebels emerged from the undergrowth and began to make their way towards the wages truck, while the ghosts or monkeys howled and the birds screamed.

Both the driver and his bodyguard were still sitting in the cab too terrified to move, as the men approached. A huge man known as El Toro ordered both of them to get out. The driver almost fell out of the vehicle in his haste to obey but then seemed to have difficulty standing and ended up kneeling in front of El Toro where, fearing he would be summarily executed, he began pleading for his life. His passenger, a National Guardsmen, remained sitting in the vehicle. El Toro ignored the driver and walking to the near side window of the truck motioned to the other man to get out. It was then that the soldier suddenly sprung to life. Throwing open the door he leapt from the cab holding an M16 which must have been on full automatic. Rafino who had been walking behind Juan hardly had time to register what was happening, let alone react, when he felt an enormous blow to his chest that lifted him off his feet and flung him backwards. He had the odd sensation of falling, as if down a mine shaft and then the blackness became oblivion and he joined the dead. Miraculously no one else was hit though a bullet passed through the sleeve of El Toro's shirt grazing his arm. The guardsmen himself died even as Rafino fell, killed by a single shot from Juan which blew away the side of the man's face.

After this incident the rebels gathered round to look at their fallen comrade, until El Tigre who had personally oversaw the ambush, ordered that Rafino's body be buried in the undergrowth. The men detailed to do this had just finished when someone found a monkey which must have been killed by a stray bullet and which was dragged over to the wages truck where it was left draped over the steering wheel with a cap taken from the dead National Guardsmen over its head. A few of the men laughed though not El Toro or the driver of the wages truck who joined the Front but was later to die while undergoing questioning by the Brigadas Especiales Contra Actos de Terrorismo.

(2)

Miguel Hortez entered Colonel Escobar's office. The colonel was looking sombre. 'Ah Captain, I am sorry to summon you at this time of the day but the wages truck to Sierra Plata has failed to return, as has the escort we provided for it. Apparently our glorious Air Force is unable to spare an aircraft to fly over the area,' the contempt in the colonel's voice was unmistakeable. 'Nevertheless,' he continued, 'we need to find out what has happened, while avoiding being sucked into a possible ambush.' He got up from behind his desk and walked over to the map on the wall. 'As you know after the Río Lamento,' he jabbed a finger at a place on the map, 'there is only one road to Sierra Plata. If there has already been an ambush or if the rebels are now waiting for us, as I suspect they well may be, it will be somewhere along here'. He traced the road with his finger, then stood looking at the map in silence. Miguel Hortez wondered if he was expected to say something but as he could think of nothing, he joined the colonel in his silent contemplation of the map. From where he was standing however, he found it difficult to see any real detail and his eyes strayed to the faded patch on the wall where a photograph of the president used to be.

'We do not have the time to mount a proper foot patrol,' the colonel was saying, 'or try to outflank any possible enemy but I need you to locate the wages truck and at the same time try to ascertain if there is an ambush awaiting us.' He gave Miguel Hortez a look of appraisal. Apparently satisfied by what he saw he said, 'Take Sergeant Becerra with you and leave the city immediately after the curfew ends. You will be travelling in a civilian truck and you will not wear uniforms. You need to look as much like civilians as possible. You will of course take your weapons in order to defend yourselves if you have to but your mission is reconnaissance. Do you understand?'

'Yes, Colonel.'

'I will personally lead the company that follows. You will have twenty-four hours start. We will rendezvous at the Río Lamento. How you carry out your reconnaissance I leave to you to act as conditions determine but what I suggest is that once you have located the wages truck or any survivors of the platoon that accompanied it, you drive on past them for a couple of kilometres, hide the truck and then make your way back to the river on foot scouting out the land as you go. If there are rebels lying in ambush it is of the utmost importance that you are not seen. If we know roughly where they are, we can hunt them down and kill them.' The colonel paused, 'have you any questions?'

Miguel Hortez thought for a few moments and then said, 'Both Sergeant Becerra and I have had training for a mission of this type but I need time to think. At the moment I have no questions but I would like to be able to come back to you if I need to?' To his surprise Miguel Hortez saw a faint smile appear on the face of Colonel Escobar.

'You are an intelligent and thinking soldier, Hortez,' the colonel said, 'that's why I chose you for this assignment.' The smile began to fade almost as quickly as it had appeared. 'And yes, you may speak to me before you go if you need to. Meanwhile we have work to do. Go to it, Captain. Sergeant Ortega will tell you where you are to pick up the truck and arrange for you to receive anything you need. That's all. Good luck Captain.'

'Thank you, Sir.'

(3)

They left the city in the relative cool of the dawn. The truck Sergeant Ortega had commandeered from somewhere had been checked over by mechanics but was old and battered. The red of its doors, contrasted with the rest of the cab which was mottled by brown rust patches and its suspension betrayed signs of hard use though the engine still ran sweetly enough. Unshaven, with their grubby clothes and straw hats, Miguel Hortez and Sergeant Becerra could pass for agricultural workers, though only from a distance. They lacked the gauntness of the undernourished and without the straw hats, their military haircuts made them immediately recognisable as soldiers.

Miguel Hortez was content to leave the driving to Sergeant Becerra. For the first three hours they drove in silence. The two men had known each other for years and despite their difference in rank, were firm friends. Their wives too had become friends and occasionally they all spent an evening together; eating, drinking and talking as two couples with children do but now both men kept their thoughts to themselves, each knowing full well what they were likely to find when they came across the missing convoy.

Ahead of them they could see the lush green of the highlands beyond the Río Lamento; the mountains a sharp contrast to the dusty but fertile coastal plain they were beginning to leave behind them. It was already becoming hot. To their left the lake shimmered in the sunlight.

'Pull over, Roberto. I will drive for a while.' The truck came to a stop and the men changed places. As the road continued its steady climb towards the mountains the sun grew higher in the sky and the temperature in the cab rose with it.

Eventually they came to the Río Lamento where they stopped to rest before moving on again towards the Valley of Ghosts and the beginning of the forest road that lead to the little mining town of Sierra Plata. Here the road narrowed and became more potholed and even more dusty. Roberto was again driving. Miguel was sitting with his M16 on the floor beside him. Roberto's rifle was wrapped in an old shirt behind the driver's seat and both men had side arms tucked into their belts beneath their shirts.

It was the Jeep they saw first but despite their experience of war it took both of them a moment to realise what they were looking at. A huge swarm of vultures all but obscured the outline of the vehicle.

'Oh mother of God!' instinctively Roberto began to slow down.

'Keep moving!'

As they drew alongside the Jeep the vultures reluctantly moved off, hissing at them as they drove past the Jeep and its remaining occupants. Roberto glanced at Miguel; briefly their eyes met but neither man spoke.

Seven hundred and fifty metres ahead, the wages truck stood undamaged apparently empty, its doors closed. As they got nearer however, they were able to make out the grotesque silhouette slumped forward over the steering wheel, its cap pulled down over one eye.

'Bastards!' muttered Roberto.

Next they passed the remains of the truck in which the soldiers, some of whom they had known, had died. Neither man said anything. They had gone another fifty metres when there was a single shot and Roberto's head exploded, showering Miguel with blood and brain tissue. Grabbing at his M16 he threw open the door and dived out of the truck but the rifle was torn from his grasp as it jammed in the opening and Miguel, who landed badly, found himself rolling down a scrub-covered slope littered with small boulders one of which all but broke his left arm. The next moment he was up and running, zigzagging through the scrub and boulders towards the shelter of the trees. Bullets whistled past him as he ran. He made the treeline, crashing through the undergrowth that lashed his face and body. He stumbled on deeper into the darkness of the forest. Behind him, hidden by the trees on the other side of the road, Juan lowered his weapon.

(4)

Miguel Hortez bent over, his hands on his knees panting. After a moment or two he straightened up and listened. The forest was eerily silent. From somewhere in the direction of Sierra Plata came the sound of birds and another sound he could not identify but that he thought sounded like insane laughter. Then he heard the voices. They were coming after him. At the same moment he became aware that he no longer had the Smith and Wesson tucked into his belt and that his face was covered in blood. He wiped his face with his hand and then realised it was not just blood but part of Roberto's brains as well. He stifled the cry that rose involuntarily in his throat. The front of his shirt was similarly covered but with dust and dirt as well. He wiped at that but only succeeded in making the smeared mess worse. After wiping his hands on the ground he looked about him trying to orientate himself. He knew he had to get back to the Río Lamento, that this lay off to his right and that to get there he would have to leave the cover of the trees. He would be travelling over scrubland, downhill with the sun beginning to go down behind him and the rebels behind and above him.

It could hardly be worse, he thought, and even as he stood there thinking, he could hear them closing in on him.

He turned and began to make his way east in the

rough direction of the river. His heart rate had returned to normal but his body felt the same as it had done after the truck hit him, though this time it was his arm rather than his leg that really hurt.

Well that's all right, he thought, as he made his way between the trees, it is my legs and my wits that will get me out of this; if indeed I do get out of it. Briefly and unbidden an image of Manolita and Jaime came into his mind. He pushed the thought and his fear away and moved on. After a few minutes, he paused again to listen. His pursuers were not as close as before and slightly off to the left. He decided that they must have thought he would go deeper into the forest but then he heard one of them off to his right. They had fanned out.

Well they would do, he thought, but they are moving slower than I am.

He guessed that they probably did not know he was unarmed, unless that is they had found his sidearm. They were being cautious and methodical. He had to take advantage of this and increase the distance between himself and them. He began to run, but slowly, being careful to avoid dead twigs and small branches and at a pace he could maintain.

No cries or shouts suggested that they could hear him. He ran on. The going was becoming easier but the forest was not as dense as before; he was approaching the scrubland beyond it. He was already soaked in sweat; nevertheless, he increased his pace slightly. He ran on and on. He considered making his way back onto the road where the going would be easier. It would be easier but potentially more dangerous. If there were more rebels lying in wait, east of the original ambush site, he would be seen and almost certainly taken prisoner or killed. He would be killed anyway if he were taken prisoner. It was just too risky. He ran on. He ran on until he could no longer run. Then he stopped to rest. After a few minutes he moved on again. He ran for what seemed like a long time but could only have been another two or three kilometres. Ahead of him lay the open scrubland. He stopped and stood looking out over the slope ahead of him. Nothing moved but still he waited, watching, listening.

He had long left his pursuers behind. Now was the time to move, to get as much distance as he could between them and him. When they came to where he now stood they too would be able to see for kilometres. They would see him. There was nothing he could do about that except to try and stay out of the range of their weapons until nightfall. When the night came he would be safe.

He started off down the slope that would eventually bring him to the river and his rendezvous point with Colonel Escobar. Once he tripped and fell but was unhurt apart from jarring his left arm that he used to cushion his fall. It would be my left arm, he thought. He ignored the pain and ran on. He saw two vultures circling off to his left. They too were searching. He looked back. Just as he did so he saw the first of his pursuers appear at the top of the escarpment. He judged them to be about fifteen hundred metres behind him.

He turned and continued running. The slope was less steep here. He stopped again and looked back. He could see a group of men, he estimated about twenty, standing where the land began to fall away but then he noticed that one man was coming down the slope after him. He moved easily and he carried a rifle in his left hand. Miguel Hortez swore softly to himself, turned and began to run again. His whole body hurt but especially his left arm and he was tiring fast but he kept running. It occurred to him that the descent favoured him in that it made it easier for him to keep moving provided of course that he did not fall. Then he stumbled and almost fell. He paused, looked at his watch and saw there was almost another hour until nightfall. He looked behind him. The man was still there perhaps a little closer, it was hard to tell but he moved with the easy grace of a coyote, effortlessly. Again Miguel cursed and turned and ran.

He ran for his life. Leaping from rock to rock, from one rock outcrop to the ground. Dodging cacti and larger boulders that blocked his way. He lost all sense of time until he became aware that the light had begun to fade. It was becoming difficult to see but then he saw the river. It was less than a kilometre away. He stopped to look behind him. He could not see the man who for the last hour had relentlessly chased him down. Then suddenly he saw him again. He was closer, within range. The man stopped and raised his weapon; Miguel began to run. A bullet ricocheted off a rock beside him. He ran on, waiting for the next shot but it did not come. He glanced over his shoulder. The man was gaining on him. He tried to increase his speed but it was impossible. He was approaching the point of collapse but still he staggered on. The light was fading quickly now. If he was lucky once his pursuer was no longer able to see him he could go off to the left or right. Then if he moved quietly enough he might be able to shake him off, to lose him in the darkness, but he knew he was running out of time. The man was already within range and catching up with him fast.

Summoning the very last of his remaining strength he willed himself to keep moving. He came to a gully about a metre and a half wide. In the fading light he could just make out a large flat boulder that offered a possible landing place in the darkness below but a split second before he jumped a bullet slammed into his left shoulder, spinning him round, and he fell sideways missing the stone and landing on his back. The impact knocked the remaining breath out of him. He lay there for a few seconds unaware of how badly he was injured; he tried to get up but his left arm lay limp and useless beside him and then in a moment of fear unlike any he had ever known before, he realised he could no longer use or feel his legs and that his spinal cord was broken.

He lay there gasping for breath. He could hear his pursuer getting closer. Miguel Hortez looked for somewhere to hide. He managed to roll over onto his right-hand side and then using his right forearm, he dragged his broken body further into the shadows. He could hear his pursuer moving through the undergrowth above. The man was moving slowly now. Miguel Hortez tried looking about him but a gasp of pain escaped his lips as his left shoulder came into contact with the ground. Somehow he managed to prop himself up on his right elbow. Then the figure of a man appeared at the top of the gully, outlined against the last light of the day. The man stood looking down at him.

Miguel said, 'How did you know we were soldiers?'

The man just stood there looking at him. At last he said, 'The man your sergeant took the truck from is known to the Liberation Front. He told us the army had come and taken his truck. Our men guessed it might be used on some sort of reconnaissance mission. One of our supporters ran the curfew and came to warn us.'

Miguel Hortez was still digesting this piece of information when the man again raised his gun to point it directly at him. Miguel said, 'I have a wife and child.' The silence of the night engulfed them. He waited. The terrible fear he had felt when he first realised he was paralysed had gone. Now he waited calmly for death.

From somewhere off to their right a coyote barked into the stillness. Another answered it. Then the man said, 'Are you National Guard or a member of the Brigadas Especiales?'

'The National Guard.'

'You are not lying to me?'

'No, I am not lying to you. Those men are dogs,' he added.

'So are you.'

'Maybe. Maybe I am.'

'You are not going to beg for your life?'

'No.'

'What about your wife and child?'

'What about them?'

'You want to see them again?'

'Yes but you will decide whether I have any chance of that. I'm probably done for anyway,' he added, 'I broke my back when I fell and my shoulder hurts like hell.'

The man said nothing. Eventually he asked, 'Do you have a weapon on you?'

'No, I lost my sidearm.'

'I know, we found it. Do you have a knife on you?'

'No,' replied Miguel.

'And you're paralysed?'

'Yes,' Miguel's voice broke, 'from the waist down, I think.'

The man still just stood there looking down at him. Then he said, 'You are a brave man, soldier.'

'I'm just a soldier,' replied Miguel.

The man said nothing. The seconds passed. Then, laying his gun on the ground, the man began to climb down into the gully. 'If you are going to survive we need to try and stop the bleeding,' he said. 'I need to look at the exit wound.'

'Why are you doing this?' Miguel asked.

'Because you no longer pose a danger to the Liberation Front or to peace-loving people,' the man replied. Miguel Hortez said nothing. 'Roll over.' He did so. Pain shot through his body like a tidal wave. He groaned. 'I will try and stem your blood loss'. Miguel gritted his teeth as the man examined his back. 'It looks as if the bullet may still be in your body. Roll over again.' Miguel did so. The man straightened his legs out. 'Were you reconnoitring the road?' Miguel remained silent. 'I'm asking because if you do not receive medical attention soon, whatever I try to do for you won't be enough. You'll probably die before morning anyway but if you do happen to make it through the night you'll need proper medical attention in the morning by the latest.'

Miguel Hortez said, 'I was to meet my commanding officer where the road forks down by the river at dawn.'

'How big a force?'

Again Miguel said nothing.

'Big enough, I suppose. I'll do the best I can to dress your wound and help you get down there.'

Much pain later, Miguel Hortez passed out while

being carried out of the gully. When he regained consciousness, he was lying propped up against a boulder beside the river. A silver moon was shining in a still night sky. Then a shadow moved in front of him and he saw the outline of a man in the moonlight.

'I've done the best I can for you,' the shadow said. Miguel said nothing. 'I'll leave this with you.' The man came forward and placed a water bottle down beside him. 'You'll need to drink. If you are still alive when your Colonel Escobar arrives you might just live to see your wife and child again. Adios. Vaya con Dios.' The man began to walk away.

'Vaya con Dios,' Miguel Hortez replied. 'Gracias,' he added.

The man stopped and turned to look at him before disappearing into the darkness. Miguel listened as he climbed away, back towards the Valley of Ghosts.

(5)

Miguel Hortez lay slipping in and out of consciousness. The first light of dawn enabled him to see his immediate surroundings and though he could not see the river, he could hear it. He felt terribly cold. Shooting pains in his legs augmented the constant sickening pain emanating from his shoulder and all down his left arm but other than that it was as if the lower half of his body was no longer part of him. Try as he might he could no more move his legs than he could move the rocks that lay out of reach around him. He lay as he had been left. A terrifying feeling of helplessness and loneliness assailed him. For the first time since he fell he began to wonder if perhaps it would have been better if he had died. Then he thought of Manolita. He contemplated the life that lay ahead of them if indeed he did survive but in a savage form of mercy, pain acted as an anaesthetic to thought and the horror of the full implications of his injuries.

Then Captain Miguel Hortez heard the rumble of Three Brigade's trucks as the company led by Colonel Escobar approached the Río Lamento but it was another hour before they found him. Shortly afterwards Colonel Escobar arrived where Miguel now lay on an army stretcher.

'Don't give him that just yet.' The medic stood back, the syringe in his hand. 'I'm sorry to find you like this, Hortez,' the colonel said. 'What happened?'

Briefly, fighting waves of pain and nausea, the exhausted man told him.

'And you saw about twenty of them?'

'Yes, Sir.'

'But only one came after you and it was he who shot you and then brought you here to the river?'

'Yes.'

'Do you know why he didn't just kill you?'

'He said I no longer posed a threat to the Liberation Front.'

The colonel seemed to consider this before asking, 'How did the rebels know you were soldiers?'

'I don't know.'

The slight hesitation before Miguel answered was not missed by the colonel, who looked thoughtfully down at him. Then he said, 'We'll do what we can for you, soldier, and we'll find those responsible and kill them.' Then turning to the medic he said, 'You can give him that now.'

The man gave him the shot of morphine and Miguel Hortez felt himself begin to float away. On the other side of a gently flowing river he saw an army truck drive past a group of people but in the truck, instead of soldiers, a row of vultures sat looking out towards him. Then he saw that the group of people were in fact his mother and father who were standing beside Manolita and that they were all waiting for him. Then his son, now older, appeared from behind them. He was dressed in the uniform of the National Guard and his hand was resting on the neck of a coyote that came forward towards him but then seemed to fade into the mist that arose from the river, and Miguel Hortez sighed and slept.

(6)

El Tigre and the rebel force had withdrawn, some into the mountains, others back towards the capital but Juan stayed behind. Now, as the company of National Guardsmen led by Colonel Escobar arrived at the site of the ambush and began to secure the perimeter, he watched and waited for his chance. Then he spotted the colonel. He knew he could only risk one shot and that he had to take it before the National Guard began their search of the mountains. Afterwards he would have to move quickly to lose the soldiers who would come after him. They would have trackers with dogs but this had been anticipated and El Toro and others had poured kerosene brought from Sierra Plata, to hinder the dogs' ability to pick up the rebels' scent, as they withdrew. Juan knew he should be able to move faster than his pursuers and, unless he was unlucky, make good his escape. He had positioned himself midway between the wages truck and the wrecked vehicle with the bodies of the burnt soldiers in it, and it was as Colonel Escobar approached the wages truck that Juan took his shot.

It was a clear straightforward shot. The colonel was virtually walking towards him, shouting at a young soldier who was standing with his back to Juan looking at the body of the dead monkey slumped over the steering wheel of the truck. Juan decided to shoot before the man obscured his line of sight but, even as he squeezed the trigger, Colonel Escobar tripped and stumbled. When Juan looked over his rifle the men were already running for cover. Juan swore softly to himself. He could not believe the colonel's luck.

Beyond the general direction he was sure the National Guard would have been unable to pinpoint his position, yet a soldier was running straight towards the place where Juan now stood. It was too late for him to begin to move back into the forest. He waited. The man came crashing through the undergrowth. He saw Juan almost immediately and stopped dead in his tracks, his rifle still across his chest as he had been holding it while he ran, its barrel pointing up into the tree canopy. For a moment the two men looked at each other, then firing from the hip, Juan shot him in the chest. With a gasp the National Guardsman sank to his knees before pitching forward onto the forest floor at Juan's feet, where he died.

Juan turned and began to run. Behind him he heard dogs barking and a man shouting orders. He guessed Colonel Escobar had already realised they were after a lone sniper, and his shooting the young soldier had effectively given away his position. However, in the brief confusion that followed and against the odds, Juan managed to slip away, though it was not until nightfall that the search for him was called off, by which time he was already half way to Sierra Plata. The elation he felt at still being alive was, however, tinged with sadness. He could not get the face of the soldier he had been forced to kill out of his mind; he had been so young. What Juan did not know, was that it had actually been the young man's eighteenth birthday.

(7)

Sergeant Ortega led the old man into Colonel Escobar's office. The man stood in front of the colonel's desk stooped and crippled by illness and a hard life. Though obviously afraid he met the colonel's gaze.

'You may sit down.' Sergeant Ortega moved a chair behind the man. Slowly and with obvious pain the man lowered himself onto it. 'I am going to ask you some questions', the colonel said. 'If you lie to me, I will hand you over to the Brigadas Especiales. Do you understand?' The man nodded. 'Answer me!'

'Yes, I understand.' The ticking of the wall clock fractured the ominous silence of the office.

'You were told your truck would be returned to you,' Colonel Escobar continued. 'The army needed your truck,' he paused, 'for a reconnaissance mission in the national interest.' The old man looked down at the floor. 'One of my men was killed and the other has been crippled for life carrying out that reconnaissance mission because the rebels knew they were soldiers. I want to know how they knew.'

The old man looked up at him. He knew with absolute certainty that his life hung in the balance. In a voice dry with fear he said, 'I don't know the answer to that.'

'You are lying,' roared Colonel Escobar bringing his fist crashing down onto the desk. Both the old man and

Sergeant Ortega flinched. 'Do you have any idea what the Brigadas Especiales will do to you if I hand you over to them?'

'I am telling you the truth and yes, I've heard what the Brigadas Especiales do to people. Who hasn't?' The old man had begun to tremble, 'but I cannot tell you what I do not know.'

A terrible stillness seemed to emanate from Colonel Escobar. Suddenly the smell of urine filled the office. The old man began to cry. 'I cannot tell you how they knew. I do not know how they knew,' he sobbed. 'I don't know. Many people know me,' he whimpered, 'could recognise my truck. They could not mistake your men for me, but apart from that, I just don't know how the rebels knew they were soldiers. I don't know. I don't know, I tell you. I just don't know.' Terror and despair filled the air, seeped into the walls and the stained floor.

'Take him away,' said Colonel Escobar. 'You are free to go,' he added. Sergeant Ortega helped the old man out of the office. 'And get someone to come and clean up in here.'

'Yes, Sir,' answered Sergeant Ortega before closing the door very quietly behind him.

CHAPTER SEVEN

(1)

From the top of the sweeping staircase the soldier led Luis and Angelina Rodrigo to the end of a long corridor where he knocked on the door and waited. After four or five seconds, a voice said, 'Come.' The soldier opened the door and motioned them to enter. He followed them inside, closing the door behind him. A man sat seemingly contemplating what appeared to be a list of names written on a single sheet of white paper that was lying on the desk in front of him.

Looking up he said, 'You wished to see me.'

'We, that is my wife and I, are trying to locate the whereabouts of our son,' Luis replied. 'He was in the university when the army entered it and he failed to return home yesterday. We understand from the news broadcasts that anyone detained by the authorities will be held by the Brigadas Especiales, so we came to ask if he is here, in your custody?'

'We do not divulge that sort of information,' the captain said curtly. 'If he is here he will either be released or you will be contacted. Meanwhile have you been to the city mortuary?'

'Our son is a student, not a rebel, and he doesn't possess a gun therefore there could be no possible legitimate reason for him to have been shot,' retorted Luis, 'and therefore,' he continued, 'there is no reason why we should go to the city mortuary to look for him. However, he *has* disappeared and we have a right to know if he is being detained and if so on what grounds.'

The man behind the desk eyed him coldly. 'You are an advocate are you not Señor Rodrigo.' It was a statement rather than a question. 'Well, I am a soldier. I assume it has not escaped your attention that we live in a country that is at war. Two members of the National Guard died when the army entered the university. They were carrying out their lawful duty and they lost their lives. So do not speak to me about rights. Here I decide what rights prisoners have and you and your wife are here because I allowed it. When you leave it will also be because I allow it. I could equally well have you thrown into a cell or shot. Do I make myself clear?'

'This is outrageous,' Luis began but then gasped as he collapsed to the floor where he lay holding his right knee with both hands. The soldier who had been standing behind him idly hefted the black baton in his right hand and let it fall softly into the palm of his left.

Turning towards the man behind the desk Angelina said, 'You bastards!' Almost imperceptibly he nodded to the soldier standing over Luis. In one smooth, almost balletic, movement the man spun round and with an arcing blow intended to smash Angelina's elbow, hit her in the ribs with his baton. Involuntarily she let out a little cry as, doubling over, she staggered backwards into a steel filing cabinet.

From his position on the floor Luis cried, 'Leave her alone!'

The soldier turned towards him and raised his baton again but the captain said quietly, 'Enough. I think the Rodrigos have learned to have more respect.' Then as Luis struggled to his feet and made his way past the soldier to his wife, the captain added. 'Take them away.' To Luis and Angelina he said, 'If we need to talk to you, we know where to find you.'

(2)

Once outside the building Luis asked, 'Are any of your ribs broken?'

'I'm not sure.' Angelina replied. 'What about your leg?'

'Well, that's not broken or I wouldn't be able to walk but it hurts like hell,' he said managing a faint smile. With difficulty they made their way down the front steps. 'The House of Dreams,' Luis muttered. 'The sick bastards!' At the bottom of the steps they turned to look back at the building.

'Did you notice the captain's eyes?' Angelina asked.

'I've never seen eyes like it. They didn't look like they belonged to a human being. What a horrible, horrible man. I think we are lucky to have got out of there alive.' Then as if suddenly realising the implication of what she had just said, she turned to Luis, 'Oh, my God. Luis, if Ramón is in there we may never see him again.'

'Don't, Angelina.'

'What are we going to do?'

'I don't know,' he replied, 'but right now we need get home and have Doctor Mendez come and take a look at you.'

'Never mind me, what about Ramón? Oh God I hope he's all right,' she sobbed. 'Oh, Madre de Dios, please don't let him be in there.'

With a mouth dry with fear Luis said gently, 'Come on Angelina.'

Slowly they made their way to the barrier. A different National Guardsman lifted it open for them. He said nothing and they said nothing to him but both Luis and Angelina heard the mocking sniggers of his companions who watched their passing with apparent amusement.

(3)

All three of them turned sharply as Cinchona entered the room. 'Forgive me Señor, Señora but there is someone asking to see you.'

'Who is it, Cinchona?'

'The young lady who left a letter for the young Master, Señora.'

'Show her in,' Angelina replied.

'I had better be going,' Doctor Mendez said to Luis.

'Yes. Yes of course. Thank you for coming, Felipe. I'm sorry I bothered you unnecessarily.'

'Not at all, Luis. It is better to have these things checked out. From what you've told me I think you were both very lucky.' Then, turning to Angelina he said, 'Avoid strenuous effort and keep your ribs strapped up for a couple of weeks. I doubt that you will do so,' he said smiling at her, 'but take the painkillers when you need them. There's no point suffering unnecessarily.'

'I'll be all right. Thank you Felipe. I told Luis not to bother you but you know what he's like – but thank you for coming so promptly. It was kind of you and I pray to God you are right about Ramón.'

'It was my pleasure. I'm only sorry to learn that Ramón has gone missing but as I said, I'll see if I can find out anything. I know some people in the army who might be able to help.'

'We'd be so grateful,' said Luis.

'Meanwhile try not to worry too much. I'm sure that if the Brigadas Especiales are holding him they will soon realise he has nothing to do with the rebels and release him.' They began moving towards the door but stopped as Cinchona ushered María into the room. The moment she saw Doctor Mendez, María's expression changed.

She looked from Doctor Mendez to Luis, from Luis to Angelina and then back at Doctor Mendez, an unmistakeable expression of naked fear on her face.

'It's all right,' Angelina said, 'there's nothing to be afraid of. You're among friends here.'

'Do you know this young woman Felipe?' Luis asked.

Before he could reply Angelina said, 'That will be all Cinchona. You may leave us. I will speak to you later.' The maid left the room taking the strained silence with her.

Turning to Luis, Doctor Felipe Mendez said, 'I've seen her somewhere before, I think, but I don't know where.'

Angelina said, 'Luis, show Felipe out. Again, thank you Felipe. I hope we see you again soon, under more pleasant circumstances.'

'I hope so too, dear lady. I hope so too. Adios.'

María stepped aside as the two men left the room. When they were gone Angelina and Maria stood looking at one another in silence. Then Angelina said, 'Now I know why my son fell in love with you. Come here, my child.' María stepped forward uncertainly. Angelina took María's hands in hers. For a few moments the two women looked at one another before Angelina said, 'I'm afraid I may have some bad news.' She saw the fear return to the young woman's face. 'It's about Ramón. We think he was in the university when the army stormed it yesterday. He did not return home last night. The last time we saw him was on Friday morning before he left to go to the university.'

'I was afraid of this,' replied María. 'That's why I came. Your maid already told me that Ramón is missing. When I saw that man I thought,' she stopped. 'Do you know him?'

'Doctor Mendez? Yes of course, he is a family friend. Why do you ask? What is it?'

María looked steadily at Angelina for a few seconds before saying, 'He has been seen entering the headquarters of the Brigadas Especiales. Many, many times,' she added, 'and often when people were being questioned.'

'How do you know this?'

'You could hear the screams.'

'I know about the screams. I meant, how do you know Doctor Mendez goes to that place?'

'I told you, he has been seen. Many times.'

Just then Luis came back into the room. Turning towards him Angelina said, 'This is María. She has just told me something you should hear. Apparently, Felipe has been seen going into the headquarters of the Brigadas Especiales and on numerous occasions. María thinks he attends the interrogations. That's what you meant, isn't it, María?'

'Yes. His visits too often coincide with times when terrible screams are heard coming from inside that building.'

'How do you know this?' Luis asked.

'Everybody living within two blocks of that place has heard the screams.'

'But you said people have seen Doctor Mendez coming and going from the House of Dreams. What people?' María remained silent looking from Luis to Angelina and then back to Luis.

Angelina said, 'We know our son is in love with you. You obviously love him. Well so do we. He is our son. You have nothing to fear from us.'

'There are some things it is safer that you do not know,' María replied quietly.

'Our son is missing!'

'Quietly Luis.'

'You are with the rebels aren't you?'

'Luis! Stop it! This young woman may have risked her life coming to ask if Ramón is safe.'

'And possibly placed us all in danger.'

'It is Ramón who is in danger! If he's even still alive,' Angelina sobbed.

'Oh forgive me Angelina. I'm sorry. I'm so sorry. Angelina, María, forgive me.'

'I think I had better leave,' said María quietly.

'No. No please stay. I'm so sorry, young lady. That was unforgivable of me but we are both so worried about Ramón, especially after our experience at the hands of those bastards in their so-called House of Dreams.'

'You've been to the House of Dreams?' asked María incredulously.

Angelina said, 'Ramón's father and I went there to ask if they were holding Ramón but they wouldn't even tell us that. In fact they beat us up a little. That's why Doctor Mendez was here. We've known him for ages. Well, we thought we knew him,' she added bitterly.

They lapsed into a poisoned silence. It lapped at their grief and fuelled their fear. It was María who broke the silence. 'I should not stay much longer anyway. It may not be safe. I'm afraid you are probably already in great danger. That man, Doctor Mendez, knows I know about him. He saw it in my face. He will suspect I am with the Front. He is a very dangerous man to know and even more dangerous to be known by. He is a friend, if such people are capable of friendship, of the captain in charge of the House of Dreams, a really bad man, a monster, one of General Gomez' butchers. A man the Front has wanted to kill for a long time.'

'I can understand that,' muttered Luis. Angelina looked at her husband and then at María.

'War makes victims or killers of us all,' María said.

'So it would seem,' said Angelina sadly. 'So it would seem.'

Luis looked as if he was about to say something but then seemed to change his mind. Turning to María he said, 'You will always be welcome here young lady. I'm deeply sorry and ashamed for what I said just now. Forgive me. Whatever has or hasn't happened to our son, he was lucky to meet you. I hope with all my heart that we will all be together in happier times, when this terrible war is over. Meanwhile you had better go, as you say, but there will always be a place for you here. If it is unsafe to come here, we will try to leave a vase on the windowsill of the study. You can see it from the other side of the street.'

'Thank you and thank you for your kind words. I too hope that we will all live to see our country awake from this nightmare. Meanwhile, I will of course see if I can find out what has happened to Ramón.' She paused, 'I'm afraid I dare not go to the city morgue for you,' her voice cracked, 'the National Guard watch all who go there.' She wiped away a tear. 'He may still be alive. I pray for all of us, that he is.'

'I will go to the mortuary,' said Luis quietly.

'Let me kiss you before you go,' said Angelina holding out her arms to María. The two women hugged and kissed one another as the tears flowed freely down their cheeks. 'Be careful María. Stay safe for us as well as for Ramón.' They clung to each for a few more seconds before Angelina went and rang the bell for Cinchona.

Luis and Angelina watched María in silence as she turned and followed Cinchona out of the room. 'Vaya con Dios,' whispered Angelina into the silence before allowing Luis to put his arm around her shoulder.

(4)

'Captain Hortez is in the room on the left at the end of the corridor, Señora. He is expecting you,' the young National Guardsman said stiffly.

'Thank you.' For a moment Manolita stood looking down the silent passage. It was good that it had been Colonel Escobar who had first told her about the extent of her husband's injuries. He imparted courage by expecting it, by taking it for granted that she would be brave because that was what her husband needed from her, just as the army had needed it from him. The difference now was that in their own way they were both going to have to face their tragedy alone, like two shipwrecked swimmers in a shark-infested sea. If Colonel Escobar knew this he had not shown it. What he would have been surprised to realise was that, while it was courage that Manolita needed as she walked down the short corridor, it was love that would allow the Hortez family to embark on a new life after the abrupt ending of Miguel Hortez' military career.

Manolita knocked lightly on the door and, without waiting, quietly entered the room. Miguel was sitting in a wheelchair looking up out of the window at the sky. She stood looking at him, waiting. After a few seconds he turned to face her. She gasped. He seemed to have aged twenty years in the ten days since she had seen him. Suffering had etched new lines in his face but it was the look in his eyes that broke her heart and her resolve and made her cry. Moving forward she knelt beside the chair and laid her head on his good arm, while sobs convulsed her whole body.

When eventually she looked up into his face, he said,

'I can no longer be a man for you, Manolita. It would have been better for all of us if I had died but I wanted so much to live, to see you and Jaime again. It was a madness before I understood how our lives would be.'

'I still love you Miguel and you are still Jaime's father. He needs you too, as I do. We can still love each other. There could never be another man for me Miguel, you know that. Somehow we will manage. We still have each other. Alegra has lost Roberto but you are still alive. We still have each other. We love one another, that's all that matters. Please Miguel, do not look at me like that.'

'Like what, my love?'

'With such sadness. Miguel please, we still have each other and our son. I thank God that you are still alive. Please, I need your love, not just the body of a man, and Jaime needs his father. We both love and need you, Miguel.'

'What good am I, as I am now, Manolita?'

'You will have a pension. We can survive. You are brave and resourceful; we can make a life for ourselves. I will no longer have to live with constant fear, wondering each time you walk out of the door if you will be coming back. For us the war is over. We can begin a new life. By God's grace we may still have many years of life ahead of us. You cannot leave us now.'

For a few seconds Miguel stared at the floor before saying, 'You ask a lot of me Manolita but I will not leave you though you will be free to leave me should you ever wish to. I would not have you stay with me out of pity. I could not live with your pity but if we are to really try this, you must cry no more because each sob you utter is like a lash and your tears are salt in the wounds. But if this is what you truly want how could I deny you your wish?'

Manolita heard the love in his voice and looked up at him but had to move slightly because a ray of sunlight had moved across the room and now shone directly into her face. When she could again see his face she was amazed to see that the sadness had gone from his eyes.

(5)

The bodies were lying beside the road. There were three of them, two females and one male. The two young women were naked; the young man still had his trousers on though they were soaked with blood but all three bodies displayed the unmistakable signs of torture.

The two men looked at one another. 'Why did you stop?' the young man asked. 'We cannot help them.'

'We cannot just leave them here,' the old man said. 'Their families will want to bury them properly.'

'We will draw attention to ourselves.'

'We can put them into the back of my truck. I will take them to the city mortuary.' The young man looked away. 'If anyone asks I will just say I found them beside the road which is of course true but I will need your help to get them into the back of my truck.'

'All right.'

'Are they the first dead people you have seen?' the old man asked.

The young man shook his head. 'No, but not like this.'

For a few moments more they stood unable to draw their eyes away from the horror that confronted them before the old man said, 'Come on, let's get it done. Move your truck. I'll reverse so we do not have to carry the bodies so far,' he limped away towards his truck.

Gently they picked up the mutilated body of the first young woman. She must have been beautiful once, the old man thought, before someone had gone to work on her with a knife.

When they had put all three bodies into the back of the old man's truck he said, 'It's lucky we happened to find them.' The young man looked at him in surprise. 'They must have been dumped here last night. If they had been out in the sun for a few days, it would have been much worse, unless of course the vultures found them first.'

'How could they do that and to women too?' the young man said. There were tears in his eyes.

'Their suffering is over now. There is no shame to cry for others,' the old man said gently. 'Now you know why we fight,' he added.

The young man remained silent for a few seconds before muttering, 'Yes. Yes I do.'

'You can drive on ahead if you like,' the old man said. 'My truck will make it back to the city.'

'It's all right, I will follow you.'

'Gracias.'

'I'm sorry about earlier,' the young man said.

'It was not an easy thing to find.' Looking into the young man's face he added, 'They are with God now. We are both just lucky they were not members of our families.'

'But to die like that!' The young man looked as if he might be sick again. 'That first one. I wonder if she was still alive when they did that to her?'

'Her suffering is over now. They are all at peace now. Remember that and put this out of your mind. Put it out of your mind now!' The old man's voice had a hard edge to it.

(6)

Though also rebuilt after the earthquake, the city mortuary was, in contrast to the new National Theatre, an ugly utilitarian structure resembling a small factory rather than a municipal building. Doctor Felipe Mendez had telephoned to say that he had been unable to learn anything from his contacts in the army, so Luis and Angelina were left not knowing if Ramón was alive as a prisoner in the House of Dreams, was already at the city morgue or was to become one of the many who just disappeared forever and without trace. Thus they went virtually every other day to the mortuary to see if his body was there.

In the immediate aftermath of the storming of the university they were among many who walked down the lines of bodies laid out in the courtyard but as the days passed they became members of a dwindling little group who regularly came with a mixture of hope and dread and left sickened by the smell of decomposition, their hunger unabated, their grief still raw.

It was on their eleventh such visit just as they were about to leave that a battered old truck stopped outside the gates. Still holding handkerchiefs to their faces, they watched as an old man got out of the cab and made his way towards the entrance of the building. He limped past them bent over as if carrying an invisible load. Luis and Angelina moved on down the last line of bodies and had just come to the end of it when the old man emerged from the building followed by two men carrying a stretcher. They walked slowly behind him, allowing him to lead them to his truck.

'Come on,' Luis said gently, 'he's not here.'

With a mixture of reluctance and relief Angelina followed as they too began to walk towards the road. The old man's truck stood partially blocking the entrance to the mortuary compound. In the sunlight something about the original red of its cab door reminded Angelina of dried blood as it shone against the brown rust on the rest of the truck's cab. The two men had just lifted the body of a young woman onto the stretcher and passed them on their way back into the courtyard as Luis and Angelina drew near to the back of the truck. The old man stepped forward but even as he did so Luis glimpsed the two remaining bodies that lay in the back of the truck. But before he had time to even turn towards her, Angelina let out a wordless piercing scream and pushed past him. It was only then as he looked again into the back of truck that Luis even recognised the body of his own son. Ramón's bruised and battered face was twisted in a hideous grimace of agony, his mouth open as he had died.

'Ramón!' howled Angelina. 'Ramón, my beautiful boy, my child,' she sobbed. 'Oh, what have they done to you?'

Luis stood frozen in shock and disbelief unable to reconcile what he saw with the little boy who had looked up at him laughing into his face as he walked beside his young wife in the early days of their marriage, in the days of quiet efficient tyranny. In the days before the terror erupted like a grumbling volcano, spewing death and misery with hitherto unimaginable savagery over the land of poets and dreamers.

'Ramón. Ramón,' Angelina was repeatedly doubling forward and straightening up again as she gripped the back of the truck. The old man stepped forward and gently tried to lead her away but she pulled herself free and turning to Luis cried, 'Luis! Look what they have done. Look what they did to our son.' Tears were streaming down her face and she seemed to be having difficulty breathing as she now stood looking at him imploringly.

Luis became aware of his heart thumping in his chest. The old man said, 'Señor, Señora. I will bring your son home to you.' Both Luis and Angelina turned towards the old man as if only now becoming aware of him. 'Go home now. Tell me where you live. I will bring your son home to you.' At this Angelina slowly sank to her knees. Both men followed her down, each holding one of her arms. Her body sagged as she knelt on the ground; her head lowered, her eyes closed as if in prayer. The two men looked at one another. 'I am sorry, Señor.'

Luis nodded.

Gently the two men helped Angelina to her feet. She stood between them, her head still bowed, staring with unseeing eyes into the past. 'Take your wife home now,' the old man spoke softly as if to a child. 'Tell me where you live. I will bring your son to you.' Luis tried to tell him but no sound came from his mouth. He tried again but the same thing happened. The two men's eyes met. 'Take a deep breath. There is no hurry. Breathe deeply.' Luis did as he was told. Eventually he managed to speak. The old man repeated the address. 'I will be there within the hour,' he said.

Luis thanked him and led Angelina away towards their car. They walked slowly, each supporting the other. The old man watched them go as, reaching out a hand to the back of his truck, he too lowered his head only raising it again when he heard the two stretcher bearers returning for the body of the mutilated young woman that still lay beside that of Ramón Alfonso Rodrigo.

(7)

They came in the early hours of the morning, the day after Ramón's funeral. Luis awoke with a start. Angelina was already up and standing by the window. 'It's the army,' her voice was flat, emotionless. Even as he leapt out of bed a terrific crash told Luis that the front door had given way. He heard shouts and the sound of men running up the stairs. He just had time to pull on his trousers before soldiers burst into the room.

'What is the meaning of this?' he demanded. By way of reply the soldier nearest him clubbed him to the floor with the butt of his rifle. He was still on all fours when he heard Angelina call out, 'I love you, Luis.'

Looking towards the door he saw a soldier dragging her out of the room. He tried to call out after her but the words came out like the unintelligible babble of an infant's attempts at speech. The next moment he felt himself being roughly pulled back onto his feet as he spat blood and fragments of teeth from his mouth.

Another National Guardsman grabbed his other arm. 'Give us any trouble and we will really hurt you. Now move!' They pushed him through the bedroom doorway ahead of them. As he began his descent of the stairs he suddenly heard screaming coming from the direction of Cinchona's room but the sound ended as abruptly as it had begun.

As he came out of the house he saw that Angelina was

already in the back of a vehicle parked outside the front entrance. It did not look like a military vehicle but more like a delivery van without windows though with a very solid looking rear door. He just had time to see a military truck standing on the street beyond it when one of the soldiers behind him shouted, 'Get in!'

He scrambled into the back of the van. Angelina was sitting on the floor. 'Are you badly hurt?' she asked. He shook his head unconvincingly. Angelina reached forward and placed her hand on his wrist. 'You poor dear.'

Outside one of the soldiers shouted, 'Silence! Prisoners are not permitted to talk to one another.' Luis and Angelina exchanged glances before looking back out through the open door of the vehicle. Unlike most of the previous week, the day promised to be fine. The sky was already blue with white clouds drifting away to southwest. A few moments later they saw Cinchona being brought towards the van. She was still in her chemise, which was torn and she was sobbing as she held the garment to her. She looked terrified and had obviously been severely beaten. The soldier with her pushed her roughly into the back of the van where she crawled away from the light like a small wounded animal. Luis watched as his wife moved across to where Cinchona cowered whimpering and, putting her arms around her maid, pulled her to her like a mother comforting a child. The next moment they were plunged into darkness as the truck's door was slammed shut.

CHAPTER EIGHT

(1)

The unsuspecting Doctor Mendez braked and cursed as the old truck pulled out in front of him. He gave the driver a long angry blast from his car's horn. Then, as it failed to move, he selected reverse with the intention of giving himself enough room to drive round it. It was only as he looked in his rear view mirror and saw the car immediately behind him that he suddenly became afraid. A moment later his driver's door was wrenched open and he found himself staring into the barrel of a gun.

'Make any noise or sudden movement and you are a dead man. Say 'yes' if you understand.' Felipe Mendez looked into the eyes of the man holding the gun; they were looking straight into his own. The barrel of the gun moved down, pointing at his chest. Juan's face was impassive. 'Keep your hands on the steering wheel. Do you understand?'

'I understand. I mean yes. Don't shoot.'

'Good, now get out of the car. Move slowly and don't try anything. *I will* use this.'

Obediently, Doctor Mendez climbed slowly out of his car. As he straightened up he was spun round from behind and pushed towards the open door of the car parked behind his own. The car's engine was running quietly. He had the fleeting impression of the vehicle being peculiarly small before realising it was because its driver was absolutely huge. As he climbed into the back, he was surprised to find a young woman sitting there. He recognised her instantly. 'You! I thought so.'

'Silence!' Felipe Mendez looked at the driver. The man was watching him in the driver's mirror.

Then Juan slipped in beside him. 'Put your hands between your knees. Keep them there and keep quiet.' Doctor Mendez did as he was told. The car reversed and then pulled smoothly and unhurriedly around his own vehicle.

'Where are you taking me?'

'If you utter another word or so much as twitch you will be sorry,' Juan replied. 'Now nod if you understand and keep quiet.' Doctor Mendez nodded then turned to look at María who was looking straight ahead. 'Eyes to the front!' He did as he was told. 'Now close your eyes and sit exactly as you are now.' Again he did as he was told.

Doctor Mendez felt María move beside him. He felt a pair of spectacles being put gently on his face. Startled he opened his eyes but all he could see was a little light coming from the sides.

'Put your hands back between your knees.'

He did so. He guessed the spectacles were meant to look like dark sunglasses only these prevented him seeing virtually anything at all. The car moved unhurriedly along. No one spoke. Never in his life had Doctor Felipe Mendez felt so afraid. He began to sweat. After about three-quarters of an hour, the car left the road and drove along a bumpy track. After a while it slid to a stop. He heard the kerbside back door open and felt the man beside him get out.

'Get out.'

He did so. He heard the other door open and then close. He guessed María had got out of the car too.

Juan said, 'Gracias amigo. Vaya con Dios.'

'De nada, it is nothing comrade,' the driver's voice was deep and gravelly as befitted his huge frame. 'Viva la revolución!'

'Viva la revolución!' replied Juan.

Doctor Felipe Mendez heard the car move slowly away. Then he felt something like a rake or broom handle touch his hand.

'Hold that and follow it.' He did as he was told. María led the way. The sun beat down on the three of them. After a short while, they entered an old disused barn with a rusted corrugated iron roof.

'You can take the glasses off now. Go and sit over there on that chair.' Felipe Mendez took off the spectacles and saw the chair in front of a few rusty pieces of farm machinery. He walked over to it and sat down.

Both Juan and María stood watching him. Juan had the gun by his side. He said, 'I am going to ask you some questions. Depending on how you answer them you will either live or die. Do you understand?'

'Yes. I understand.'

'You are familiar with the headquarters of the Brigadas Especiales are you not?'

'I wouldn't say I am familiar with it but I have been there,' Felipe Mendez replied.

'For what reason?'

'My services as a doctor were required to tend a prisoner.'

'Just one?'

'I have been there a few times. On some occasions I had to attend to more than one person.'

'What was the nature of their injuries?'

'It varied. Gunshot wounds mainly.'

'Mainly gunshot wounds?'

'Yes.'

'What other injuries did you have to treat?'

'Sometimes prisoners were ill.'

'Ill?'

'Yes.'

'Did you ever have to treat people who had been tortured?'

After the smallest hesitation Doctor Mendez said, 'On a few occasions I had to give pain relief to people who had been severely beaten.'

'Prisoners?'

'Yes.'

'Were you ever present while prisoners were beaten?'

'No.'

'Never?'

'No.'

'Are you sure?'

'Of course I'm sure.'

'You liar!' screamed María.

'María!' Juan's voice was like a whiplash. She turned towards him trembling. 'I told you to remain silent. Either you remain silent or I must ask you to go outside.' His voice, though quiet again, was still the voice of command.

For a few moments she stood staring at him defiantly before turning away to hide her tears. 'I'm sorry, Juan.'

Doctor Mendez said angrily, 'I object to being called a liar by that girl. How could she possibly know when I was attending prisoners and under what circumstances?'

'Silence!' roared Juan. Doctor Mendez looked as if he were about to reply but thought better of it. María's sobs filled the barn. 'You! Stay where you are.' Without taking his eyes off the doctor, Juan went over to María and placed his free hand on one of her heaving shoulders. Softly he said, 'Go outside.'

She turned her tear-streaked face towards him. 'No please; I have to stay. Please, Juan.'

For a moment he stood looking into her face before saying gently, 'As you wish.'

He walked back and stood looking down at Doctor Felipe Mendez. For a few seconds the two men looked at each other in silence, then Juan said, 'I will ask you again; were you ever present while prisoners were beaten or otherwise ill-treated?'

'No. I swear to you. Never.'

'Were you ever elsewhere in the building while prisoners were being tortured?'

'I don't know. I may have been.'

'Did you ever hear screams that suggested that prisoners were being tortured?'

'I sometimes heard noises but I was not sure what they were or what caused them,' Doctor Mendez replied.

'Did you hear screams?' persisted Juan.

'I may have done but prisoners often shouted to one another or at their guards.'

'Shouted?'

'Yes.'

'But you never heard screaming?'

'I've already told you. I may have done. I'm not sure.'

Juan glanced at María. She was looking straight at Doctor Mendez with a mixture of incredulity, utter revulsion and raw, raw grief. Looking back at the doctor Juan noticed how he avoided looking at her. Suddenly and unbidden the face of the young National Guardsman he had shot while escaping from the Valley of Ghosts flashed into his mind. With a weary sadness he asked, 'Where were you when you treated the prisoners?'

'What do you mean, where was I?'

'Where did you treat them; in their cells or somewhere else?'

'What difference does it make?' retorted Doctor Mendez.

'Just answer the question.'

'I've had enough of this!'

'Oh you have, have you?' A dangerous anger had edged into Juan's voice. 'Perhaps you have also had enough of living too?'

María said, 'He's lying Juan. Can't you see he's lying? We already know…'

'María!' Then more softly, 'María, please.'

'I'm sorry, Juan.' Her voice was little more than a whisper.

Turning back to the doctor, Juan said, 'Doctor Mendez I will ask you just once more, where were you when you treated injured prisoners?'

'In their cells.'

'Did you ever hear screaming coming from other cells?'

'No.'

'Never?'

'No. Never.'

'From elsewhere then?'

'No. I've already told you that.'

An ominous silence filled the barn. From somewhere far away a bell tolled. Juan said, 'Doctor Mendez, we know you have been to the House of Dreams many times. We also know that on almost every occasion, your visits have coincided with the most terrible screams coming from that building. It would have been utterly impossible for you not to have heard them. We believe you actually attended those interrogations.'

'That's not true.'

Ignoring this, Juan continued, 'We also know that those who die during such interrogations either just disappear or their bodies are found dumped in the countryside or beside the road. They are just left for the coyotes or the vultures to find. But all the bodies that have been found by human beings bear the unmistakeable signs of having been severely tortured.'

'I've had nothing to do with anything like that,' protested Doctor Mendez, getting up.

'Sit down!'

The doctor sat down again. He was now clearly very afraid. 'You visited the House of Dreams the night after the National Guard and members of the Brigadas Especiales stormed the university,' Juan continued. 'Did you not?'

'I don't recall.'

'Well, we know you did. Among the few students who survived the actual massacre at the university and were taken to the House of Dreams was a young man named Ramón Rodrigo. Does the name mean anything to you?'

'No, should it?'

'His body was found dumped at the side of the road on the Avenida de Patriotismo. He had been tortured.'

'I've already told you, I know nothing about people being tortured or about that young man and I do not know the names of any of the prisoners.'

'But you know Captain Trujilla.'

'Of course I do. He is the officer in charge.'

Juan again glanced across at María before saying, 'We know that you drink with Captain Trujilla and we know more about him than you could ever guess.'

'I have only drunk with him after I have had to attend to the injured. I had no choice. Just as I had no choice but to go to the House of Dreams when summoned to do so.'

'Enough! I have heard enough,' said Juan. 'Stand up.'

Doctor Mendez did so. He was trembling and had soiled his trousers. Juan said, 'Doctor Felipe Mendez, for complicity in the torture and the murder of Ramón Rodrigo and probably countless others, you will now be taken outside and shot.'

At this María began to sob again. For his part Doctor Mendez fell to his knees crying, 'No. No please you can't. I have a family. I have a wife and two children. A boy and a girl of thirteen.'

'The Rodrigos only had one child,' replied Juan, 'their son, Ramón. He was twenty-one years old. He was a student. He wasn't even a member of the Front.'

'I was not involved in his death. I swear it.'

'Get up off your knees,' ordered Juan. 'You have lived like a dog all your life. At least now try to die like a man.'

For a few moments Doctor Felipe Mendez remained motionless staring up into Juan's face before slowly getting to his feet. Juan pointed the gun at his chest. In a voice now devoid of fear Doctor Mendez said, 'I qualified as a doctor of medicine before this war began and I have treated the poor as well as the rich. I have killed no one. I do not need you to tell me how to die like a man.'

'Outside then!' Juan motioned to the doctor with the barrel of his gun.

(2)

The three of them emerged from the barn into the sunlight. 'Turn right and keep walking.' Doctor Mendez did so. The plain stretched away shimmering in the heat, towards the mountains. They walked on. A pile of freshly dug earth came into view. A shovel lay beside the freshly dug grave. 'Get in.'

Doctor Mendez did so and turned to face Juan. 'You know the Front can never win don't you?' he said.

María said, 'Juan give me the gun. Let me do it.'

'No María.'

'Let me do it for Ramón. I loved him. I loved him, Juan.'

'I know María. I know.'

'For his mother, then,' she pleaded. 'Let me do it for Angelina and his father.'

'No, María. This is for me to do,' he said. The two stood looking at one another for a few seconds before Maria turned and began to walk away.

Doctor Mendez said, 'I am sorry for the death of your young man, Señorita. If I could bring him back for you, I would.'

María stopped and stood looking at Doctor Mendez. She was no longer crying.

Juan said, 'Are you ready?'

'I am ready,' Doctor Felipe Mendez replied.

Juan raised his gun and fired. Felipe Mendez staggered back before falling half in and half out of the shallow grave. Putting down his gun, Juan pulled the dead man into place before picking up the shovel and burying his body, where he had died.

(3)

After twenty minutes the van carrying Luis and Angelina Rodrigo together with their maid Cinchona arrived at the headquarters of the Brigadas Especiales. From the walled courtyard where the van stopped, the three of them were taken towards the rear of the building. 'No one is allowed to talk here,' one of the soldiers told them. 'If you talk you will be severely punished. You better remember that.'

Once inside they were led down a long corridor with steel doors down either side of its entire length. Here they were put into identical windowless cells adjoining one another. The cells themselves were no more than two metres deep and a metre and half wide and were completely bare save for a latrine bucket opposite the door. In all three cases the foul smelling buckets still contained waste from the cells' previous occupants.

No sound came from the outside world and time passed slowly with the almost sepulchral silence made even more oppressive by groaning coming from a cell towards the end of the corridor. A few hours after the Rodrigos' and Cinchona's arrival someone called out begging for water. Measured footsteps could be heard walking down the corridor. Whoever it was had steel cleats in the heels of their boots and the sound they made echoed throughout the corridor. A metal bolt slid back and a voice said, 'You'll get water when we give you water.'

Then a voice cried out, 'No, please. Please, I just need water. No! Please.' The loud crack of a whip melded into a scream that was followed by agonised sobbing. A door clanged shut and a metal bolt slid back. The same unhurried footsteps retraced their previous echoes. Another door closed and a poisoned quiet returned to the House of Dreams.

A short while later the cleated boots came for Cinchona and took her to the far end of the corridor.

Her terrified, 'Where are you taking me?' was answered by what sounded like a vicious slap across her face. Her subsequent crying mingled with the sobbing of the whipped man until the door at the end of the corridor opened and then clanged shut. This time no metal bolt was heard sliding back. Shortly afterwards the screaming began. When at last it ended the door at the end of the corridor remained shut and Cinchona never returned along the corridor or to the house of Luis and Angelina Rodrigo.

(4)

They did not know how long it was before they came for them and, with only one electric bulb in the ceiling of each cell, neither Luis nor Angelina knew what time it was; whether it was night or day in the world outside. Both were severely dehydrated though not hungry but most of all they were surprised that their captors chose to take them to the room at the end of the corridor together. Luis' face was terribly swollen and turning purple and each wanted desperately to speak to the other but both knew that the three men accompanying them would show little mercy if they so much as breathed a word to each other.

On entering the room, it only took them a moment to confirm what it was used for. They were both aware that two of the three men who had taken them from their cells had come in with them and were standing behind them but the first thing they noticed was the big man wearing blood-spattered overalls and a large clear plastic apron that looked wet but still bore smears of blood on it. He had a brutal, ugly, unintelligent-looking face strangely like the captain's, though oddly misshapen as if seen in the rippled reflection of a stream. The captain was sitting behind a desk on which there was a carafe of water, three glasses and incongruously, a riding crop. 'So we meet again,' he said.

'What have you done to our maid,' demanded Angelina.

The captain looked surprised. The man wearing the plastic apron looked amazed but slowly a grin of anticipation spread across his face. One of the men standing behind Angelina moved but the captain shook his head slightly. 'She has been released,' he answered.

'I don't believe you,' retorted Angelina. Luis did not know whether to look at the captain or his wife and fear rendered him mute.

'I would have thought that after our last meeting you would have learned to have a little more respect,' Captain Trujilla said evenly, pouring himself a glass of water.

'For over an hour you or this monster,' Angelina said indicating the man wearing the plastic apron, 'hurt her. Everyone in the whole building must have heard her screams.'

'Then you must realise that, should I choose, we could make you or your husband scream too,' said the captain.

'I'm sure you could,' said Angelina. 'We have just buried our son. We both saw what you did to him. What more could you do to us?'

'You would be surprised,' replied the captain.

'Nothing you could do to us would surprise me,' Angelina looked unflinchingly at the captain.

For several seconds the two held each other's gaze. Luis stood helplessly, trying to stop himself from visibly trembling. The man wearing the apron and the two guards waited like dogs to be allowed to eat their food.

At length the captain looked down at a piece of paper on his desk. He said, 'We know your son was involved with a woman we know as María from the mountains. We know also that she is a member of the so called Liberation Front; that she has been to your home twice and that you have both only met her once but your son was never taken into custody by the Brigadas Especiales. Whatever has befallen him was not of our doing.'

'I don't believe that either,' retorted Angelina. 'He disappeared the day the army stormed the university. For two weeks we searched among the bodies at the city mortuary. They were all young people; almost certainly just students like our son. Then one day we just happened to be there when his body was brought in. He had not been dead long but whoever killed him had done things to him that will haunt us for the rest of our lives. Whatever you do to us, you cannot hurt us more than we have already been hurt.' For a moment her voice faltered but she continued. 'As for your María of the mountains as you call her, she and our son met and fell in love. You will have destroyed her life as well as ours.' Tears had begun to run silently down her cheeks. 'And what about our poor little maid Cinchona? She has committed no crime whatsoever. How can you live with yourself? How can you sleep at night?' Angelina began to sob. Luis, who had remained silent throughout, lowered his head as tears flowed freely down his face. They stood there broken by their grief, beyond hope, almost beyond fear. The silence in the room was deepened by Angelina's sobbing and her apparent difficulty breathing. Without thought, Luis went and put his arms around his wife. Nobody moved.

Captain Trujilla sat perfectly still, looking at them; a peculiar expression on his face. At length he said, 'You are free to go.' Again nobody moved. 'You are free to go,' he repeated. Then, 'Take them to the gate and let them go.' Still nobody moved. 'You heard me. Take them to the gate and let them go. Now. Move!'

Strong hands took Luis and Angelina by the arm and led them out through double doors at the other end of the room. In the darkness they both failed to notice the little blood-drenched corpse lying by the wall to their right.

By the gates at the entrance to the courtyard the men left them without a word. For a minute or more they both just stood there, each supporting the other, bowed like the old until raising their eyes to each other and without so much as a backwards glance at the House of Dreams they slowly made their way into the torn silence of the night.

(5)

Almost three years had passed since the death of Ramón and the disappearance of Cinchona. Three years during which the Rodrigos had grown old. Three years, during which they seldom saw María though they received regular messages from her, delivered verbally by people they had never before met and whom they seldom saw again, but they both slept badly and the nights were long. The cicadas and the sirens of the Jeeps of the Brigadas Especiales now vied not just with each other but with the increasing frequency of explosions and gunfire that could be heard across the city throughout the hours of darkness; so they were already awake the night the wounded fighter was brought to their front door.

'Forgive me Señor, Señora.'

'You!'

'Yes it is I,' the old man replied. 'A friend of María's has just been shot,' he continued. 'He needs medical attention and soon, if he is to live.'

'Luis, get out of the way and let them in.'

'Yes. Yes of course. Bring him in. Bring him in.'

'Gracias Señor, Señora.' Other figures emerged from the shadows. They carried the wounded man past Luis into the entrance hall.

'This way.' Angelina led them towards Cinchona's room at the back of the house. 'He will be safe here. Well, as safe as anyone can be in these days.'

To the men who had carried the wounded fighter, the old man said, 'Vamos, go!' Then as they turned to go, 'Be careful. You must not be seen leaving here.' The men nodded and with mumbled thanks and nods to Luis and Angelina they headed back to the front door where Luis quietly let them out.

When he returned to the Cinchona's room, Angelina was already examining the wounded man. She looked up at the two men as Luis entered the room. 'This looks very serious,' she sounded worried.

'We know a doctor who can be trusted,' the old man said. 'If the Senōra could be ill,' he suggested, turning to Luis, 'our man could visit her later today.'

'I'm sure I could manage that,' said Angelina, 'but your friend may not even be alive by the morning.'

The old man turned to look at her, his eyes were as bright as a crow's. 'Forgive me Señora. I am an old man. The world and its ways change too quickly for me to keep up with.' Then looking at them both he said, 'This was his only chance.'

'We understand,' replied Angelina. The old man glanced at Luis, who nodded.

'Whether he lives or dies,' the old man continued, 'I or someone else will return to take him off your hands as soon as it is safe to do so.' Then looking pointedly at Luis he said, 'Try and use the vase in your study window, Señor, to warn us if there is danger here.'

Both Luis and Angelina looked at him in surprise. For a moment a crooked smile appeared among the contours of the old man's face. He said, 'Even a rat must live by his wits if he is to survive.'

'We will never harm a rat again,' said Angelina.

The old man chuckled. 'Perhaps you should extend your goodwill only to those you know well,' he said.

'I will heed your advice,' Angelina replied, 'but you had better go now or would you prefer to wait until the curfew is lifted?'

Despite the situation, Luis noted that his wife's face, though still looking worried, was alive in a manner he had not seen since the death of their son.

'No Señora but gracias,' the old man said. 'It is better that I am not seen leaving here. I may be old but like the rat, I am difficult to notice in the darkness. I will be all right.'

Luis said, 'I will see you out.'

Then Angelina said, 'Forgive us but we still do not even know your name, Señor.'

The old man turned to look at her. 'You may call me Pablo, Señora. It is a name I have always much liked,' he added with a grin.

'Then Pablo, until we meet again, vaya con Dios.'

'Vaya con Dios, Señora,' the old man replied gravely. 'Vaya con Dios, Señor.'

'Vaya con Dios,' replied Luis stiffly before leading the old man to the front door where he too slipped away, a crooked man who vanished silently among the crooked shadows of the night.

(6)

The doctor arrived early, just after sunrise and soon after the curfew was over. Luis was waiting for him by the front door.

'Señor Rodrigo?'

'Yes. Are you the doctor?'

'I am. Doctor Fiestal at your service. Manolo Fiestal.'

'Luis Rodrigo. I'm so glad you are here Doctor. Come this way.' Luis led the way to Cinchona's room where Angelina was sitting beside the wounded man. She stood up as the doctor entered the room.

'Buenos dias Señora,' Doctor Fiestal said before bending over the wounded man and feeling his pulse.

'Good morning,' she replied.

'How long has he been like this?' the doctor asked as he lifted the corner of the blood-soaked dressing covering the young man's chest.

'He was like this when they brought him here,' Angelina replied.

The doctor looked worried. Hastily he rummaged in his bag, produced a syringe, filled it and slid the needle into the arm of the barely breathing man. 'His blood pressure is critically low and he has obviously lost a lot of blood though the bleeding seems to have stopped.' Having administered the injection he again took the young man's pulse. 'But he needs surgery and a blood transfusion,' he explained slowly straightening up. 'I'm sorry to have to tell you this but I am afraid I cannot help this young man, there is nothing I can do for him. He's going to die. Luckily he's not in pain. Apart from the obvious severity of his wound he has all but bled out already. He will almost certainly be dead within the next hour if not before. I'm sorry.'

Angelina gave a little gasp and turned away as tears silently began to run down her cheeks.

Doctor Manolo Fiestal looked from Angelina to Luis who was looking at his wife with a look of such sadness and concern that the doctor felt compelled to say, 'I'm sorry,' again. 'I will give him a sedative,' he added. 'It will ensure he does not suffer should he begin to regain consciousness which is most unlikely but it will ease his passing if he does. There is nothing else I can do for him.' The doctor quietly gave the dying man the injection and slowly closed his bag.

Turning towards Doctor Fiestal, Angelina said, 'Thank you for doing what you could, Doctor. It is a great comfort to know he will not suffer any more before he dies. Luckily he seemed not to suffer at all while he was with us. It just seems so sad,' her voice cracked, 'because he is so young. Excuse me.' Hurriedly she left the room.

The doctor and Luis exchanged glances. 'We lost our own son almost three years ago,' Luis said.

'I am sorry to hear that,' Doctor Fiestal said. 'This must make this even harder for you both. I'm truly sorry.'

'Thank you.'

The deep tones of silence mingled with the sadness in the room. Doctor Fiestal said, 'I could leave something for your wife, if you think it would help.'

'I think we are both beyond the reach of medication,' Luis replied, 'but thank you anyway.'

'Yes of course. I understand.'

Luis led Doctor Fiestal to the front door where, at the bottom of the steps, they parted. After the doctor had left, Luis turned back towards the house and with deep resigned sadness went in search of his wife.

(7)

Pablo returned later the same day, for the body of the young man. 'Was it safe to return so soon and in daylight too?' Luis asked looking past the old man to where his rusty old truck now stood outside their front door.

'It is safer to move during the day, Señor. Besides, what could you have done with the body?' the old man replied, 'and things have changed. This young man will explain the situation to you both,' he said, bowing slightly to Angelina as she joined her husband on the steps leading up to their front door. The old man moved to one side.

A lithe handsome man in his early forties who had been standing virtually unnoticed behind him came forward. He was carrying a wooden board under one arm. 'My name is Juan,' he said quietly. 'If we could just collect the body, Pablo can be on his way. The sooner he and the body of Edgardo are gone from here, the safer it will be for all of us.'

'Is there some danger?' Luis asked.

'There is always some danger in an operation like this Señor, but do not be unduly alarmed, we have people watching the street and we should all have time to get away if the army were to arrive, but we should not delay.'

Luis said, 'What do you mean, time to get away? We live here, this is our home.'

'I will explain everything, Señor Rodrigo but if we could first just collect the body of our comrade.'

Angelina said, 'This way then.' Luis turned and followed his wife indoors. Pablo and Juan followed. Quickly they made their way to Cinchona's room where the body of Edgardo Delblanco lay.

His face looked peaceful though already beginning to acquire the waxy look of the dead. Quickly but respectfully Juan and the old man transferred his body from the bed to the board.

'I will take the other end of that,' Luis said.

'Gracias.' The old man left the room ahead of them. Angelina was reminded of the first time she and her husband had seen him and how frail he looked in the light of day.

After they had placed the young man's body into the back of the truck, Pablo placed a tarpaulin over it and then he and Juan quickly heaped timber on top of that.

Climbing down off the back of the truck Pablo said, 'Señor, Señora, I'm sorry to have visited this trouble upon you. I'm sorry it was for nothing. I did not realise how badly he was hurt.'

'This tragedy was not of your making, Pablo,' Angelina said, 'besides you brought our son home to us. We're in your debt. I'm just sorry that this young man had to die so young.'

'It is indeed sad,' replied Pablo, 'especially as his older brother died trying to kill General Gomez.'

In a voice Luis had never heard before, Angelina said, 'What did you say his name was?'

Juan said, 'He was called Edgardo Delblanco but everyone called him El Gato.'

'El Gato,' Angelina repeated the name, 'the cat. Vaya con Dios El Gato. Vaya con Dios.'

The three men stood looking at Angelina until Juan said quietly, 'You'd better be gone, Pablo.'

The old man nodded. 'May the peace of God be with you both,' he said to Luis and Angelina.

'And with you, Pablo,' Angelina replied. 'Vaya con Dios.'

Luis remained silent but raised his hand in a gesture of farewell.

The old man turned away and climbed into the cab of his truck. It came to life with a cough before slowly pulling out of the yard. The three of them stood listening as it disappeared down the street. No gunfire greeted its departure.

CHAPTER NINE

(1)

It had long been clear to Colonel Escobar that it was just a question of time before the rebels finally overran the capital and that the war was already effectively lost. Three Brigade and the Brigadas Especiales now seldom left the city, though other brigades still ventured out into the countryside, despite it and the nights belonging to the rebels. In the capital, however, the Brigadas Especiales still chose to raid people's homes either during the hours of darkness or just after sunrise, both as a tactic of surprise and in keeping with General Gomez' strategy of *'The Iron Fist'*. A policy Colonel Escobar was now certain had more to do with attempting to terrorise the population into compliance than to avert further bloodshed. Indeed many of the casualties within the city were of people either caught in cross fire between the army and rebel fighters now operating more or less openly within the city, or, more often, of civilians just going about their everyday lives who were somehow mistaken for rebels. But despite his best efforts to protect the men under his command and to ensure they conducted themselves with restraint as far as civilians were concerned, Colonel Escobar was losing men on a more or less daily basis and the number of casualties among the civilian population was also steadily rising.

So it was that he finally decided to again confine Three Brigade to barracks, this time indefinitely. He knew that by so doing he was acting against the direct orders of General Gomez and that there would be swift and drastic consequences. Having issued the order and seen it acted upon he forbade all junior officers from approaching the headquarters and administration building. He then had Sergeant Ortega arrested and held in detention. His headquarters thus emptied, he went about booby-trapping his office and the whole of the administration building. The colonel worked quickly but methodically, completing the task in less than an hour. Finally he emptied out Sergeant Ortega's wall to ceiling filing cupboard, knocking out all the support shelves and throwing the files into the small armaments storeroom. Having examined his handiwork, he settled back to wait.

He did not have to wait long. Just before noon he saw General Gomez' car swing through the camp's main entrance and to his astonishment realised that it was without a military escort. Marvelling at the arrogance of power, he openly walked past the front window as if making his way to his office and then crouching, doubled back to the outer office where he hid in Sergeant Ortega's now empty filing cupboard.

As he expected, Colonel Johnson entered first moving fast and silently, his Ingram submachine gun at the ready. A second man followed close behind him. He too held a weapon though only a Smith and Wesson automatic. Colonel Escobar, peeping through a small crack he had made in the door, watched the gringo fire a short burst through his office door before kicking the door open.

The explosion was more powerful than he had expected and Colonel Escobar was barely conscious when he emerged from his hiding place. He need not have worried however, the outer office into which he staggered was almost completely wrecked and he could clearly see the parade ground through the enormous hole in the back wall of what had been his office. The wall facing him was covered in blood spatter. Of Colonel Johnson and the man who had accompanied him, all that remained were body parts scattered seemingly at random around the room.

A movement caught the corner of his eye. Turning he saw General Gomez silhouetted in the entrance doorway. He was covered in dust and looked dazed but he had an automatic in his hand that was pointing in the direction of Colonel Escobar. He said, 'I knew I should have had you shot, you treacherous bastard!'

'Be careful where you point that, General, it might go off.' Then raising his own weapon he said, 'Drop it,

General. Apart from the fact that your chances of hitting me from there are small, a burst from this would cut you in half.' General Gomez glared at him. Colonel Escobar could see him calculating his chances. He squeezed the trigger. General Gomez flew backwards out of the door. None too steadily Colonel Escobar made his way there and looked out. The much-feared General Gomez lay on his back; an open-mouthed little fat man with a surprised expression on his face. He lay there in the dust, his legs splayed out, his right arm outstretched with the gun still in his hand.

Men from Three Brigade were running towards him weapons at the ready. Upon seeing their colonel standing there they slowed to a stop unsure of what was expected of them, unsure what to do.

Colonel Escobar said, 'At ease, men. It's over. As your commanding officer I order you to remain on camp until I tell you otherwise. The main gates are to remain closed and you are to be ready at all times to defend this base, and no members of the Brigadas Especiales are to be allowed on camp.' He paused giving the men time to absorb the implication of this command. 'Three Brigade will no longer prosecute this war against the rebels,' he continued. 'This war was lost a long time ago. All further loss of life, whether of us, civilians or even the rebels is pointless. As members of the National Guard we will of course never surrender to anyone, but our duty was, has always been and still is, to protect our country. We cannot do that by killing yet more of its citizens. We will no longer kill our fellow countrymen unless we are forced to, to protect our own lives or those of our families. Is that understood?'

A profound silence answered Colonel Escobar. Nobody moved. It was Miguel Hortez' replacement, the newly-promoted Captain Guba who shouted, 'Yes sir,' which after a pause of no more than a few seconds was followed by shouts of 'Viva Colonel Escobar. Viva el Colonel!'

At length Colonel Escobar raised both arms for silence. The shouts subsided. Colonel Escobar stood looking at his men; they stood waiting. 'Viva Three Brigade,' he roared. 'Dismiss.'

Few of the men actually moved, instead they stood and watched in respectful silence as their colonel walked past the still smouldering administration building and out onto the middle of the empty parade ground where he stood, a lone figure looking in the direction of the mountains and up at the national flag fluttering proudly from its flagpole in the gentle onshore breeze.

(2)

Juan said, 'We have reason to believe that you have been betrayed by one of your neighbours. We expect the Brigadas Especiales to come for you, though probably not until the early morning, but one can never be sure about these things, so I suggest you pack a few clothes as quickly as you can and we will take you to a safe house on the outskirts of the city, now before the curfew comes into effect.'

Luis and Angelina looked at one another. It was Angelina who spoke. 'This is our home. Everything we have ever loved, everyone we have ever loved or been loved by, has been here. Our whole life is here.'

'I understand,' said Juan gently, 'but you have been to the House of Dreams. You know what awaits those who are taken there. No one has ever before been released twice. You will not be released a third time and we will be unable to help you should you be taken there again.' He watched as Luis and Angelina considered this. He said, 'What we would like to do is wait for them to come for you, only we will be waiting for them.'

Without hesitation Angelina said, 'Then we would like to wait here too.'

Juan looked at Luis who said, 'We will not be driven from our own home. We would both rather die here.'

Juan looked from one to the other. He understood their calmness, their resolve and its progeny of inner stillness. 'Can either of you use a gun?' he asked.

Angelina said, 'My husband used to shoot a little when he was younger, didn't you my dear.'

Juan saw the look of love that passed between them. The last time he had seen that look was when he had watched Señora Delblanco hold her husband in her arms as he died. Pushing the thought from his mind he said, 'If I cannot talk you out of this, you must at least realise that to stay after whatever happens here would be suicide. If you are determined to stay and fight you must leave with those of us who are alive when it is over. Live to fight another day. We will all join the dead soon enough.'

'Agreed,' replied Luis.

'Agreed,' echoed Angelina.

Juan smiled. 'Then if you will excuse me, I have things to arrange. I will be back.' With that he took his leave of them.

(3)

Most of the rebels arrived in heavily armed groups of three or four after dark and immediately took up defensive positions overlooking the courtyard. One of the young men, who had helped carry El Gato to Cinchona's room, explained that the plan was to allow a few members of the army to actually enter the hall before opening fire from the landing and that would be the signal to open fire generally.

Juan himself returned just after midnight together with María and a huge man with a villainous-looking face whom he introduced as El Toro and who immediately assumed command of the planned ambush. For her part, María began helping Angelina with the preparation and distribution of food for the fighters. The night wore on. They waited, the tension mounted. Daybreak came and the curfew ended. The noise of the city coming to life vied with that of the cicadas and the song of birds as the sun rose steadily in the sky. Oddly there was no gunfire. The men who were not sleeping became restless. Then suddenly the old man's truck swung into the courtyard and stopped. The driver got out. 'It is I,' he shouted. 'Don't shoot!' He lowered his hands. 'General Gomez is dead,' he yelled. 'The National Guard have withdrawn to their barracks. A notice is posted on the front gates, which says that as far as they are concerned the war is over. They will only fight to protect themselves and their families.' He stopped and stood looking up at the silent house. 'The body of General Gomez is hanging from the wall beside the main gate of the barracks,' he stopped again. 'Hello! Where are you? Are you all asleep?'

Seconds passed then the front door opened and El Toro emerged from the house, gun at the ready. The old man grinned and said, 'Don't waste a bullet on me, you mad bull, there are still plenty of Brigadas Especiales to hunt.'

'I wouldn't waste a bullet on you, you old goat,' replied El Toro, 'you could die of old age before it reached you!' Other men came out of the house and began to appear at the windows. 'Are you sure it is the body of General Gomez?' he asked.

'I am sure,' replied the old man.

El Toro turned to Juan, 'What do you think?'

'What else do you know?' Juan asked the old man.

'As I left the Plaza de los Astros a crowd was beginning to gather. There was much rejoicing and waving of flags; it does indeed appear as if the war may be over. Some of our comrades are walking openly in the streets. There are no snipers on the roofs and no military vehicles on the street and certainly no sign of the Jeeps of the Brigadas Especiales. The National Guard do indeed seem to be staying in their barracks and they have left the body of General Gomez hanging from the wall beside the main gate of their barracks. That seems to me to be a very clear statement! There is no going back for Colonel Escobar now.'

'If he's still alive,' El Toro said thoughtfully.

'I think he will be very much alive and I can go to see Colonel Escobar,' said Juan. There was a stunned silence from the men standing around them. 'Don't worry, I'm not his man, you know that.'

El Toro said, 'If that is so, how do you know he will not just kill you?'

'Firstly, that *is* so and you and all here know it,' replied Juan evenly, looking straight into El Toro's eyes. Second…'

El Toro's deep gravelly voice interrupted him. 'We know it Juan. I should not have questioned your loyalty.' Turning towards the men he said, 'I will happily give my life as forfeit if this man betrays any one of us, even under torture.'

One of the men said, 'But he might take you hostage, Juan.'

'It would hardly be a display of good faith and besides I think I know how the man thinks,' replied Juan. 'If he is still alive, as I am sure he is, he wants to save his men. I may be able to do more than just find out if he is still alive. He does not care about his own life. He has always led from the front and his men would follow him into hell itself. By the same coin, if he orders them to stand down, they will do so. Besides who else do you think would have dared to kill General Gomez? No, this was the act of a very singular man. Three Brigade have some brave men as we all know but there is only one man who could have killed General Gomez and that man is Colonel Escobar.'

The old man said, 'Juan we know you are brave but could I not be the one who goes to see if Colonel Escobar is still alive? If he is the man you say he is, he will not have me killed but even if he does I'm an old man. I've had my life, it will not matter.'

El Toro snorted and said, 'How many more men wish to go and speak with Colonel Escobar? Enough of this nonsense, if Juan is prepared to go he is the best man for the job. As he says he may be able to accomplish far more than merely find out if Colonel Escobar is still alive.' Turning to Juan he said, 'I swear before all these men that if anything happens to you, I will personally take it upon myself to kill the colonel even if it costs me my life.'

'Then we are all agreed,' said Juan.

'I think perhaps you and Colonel Escobar may find a lot to say to one another,' observed Pablo.

'Since when did you begin to think, you old goat?' El Toro said. The men gathered round laughed.

'Only after I watched you trying to do so,' retorted Pablo.

The men laughed again but uncertainly. For a moment El Toro tried to look angry but then he too burst out laughing. 'Enough of this circus. We have a use for your truck, old man.' Then addressing the men he said, 'Comrades now is our chance to hunt down the real killers of our comrades and our countrymen. The Brigadas Especiales no longer have the protection of the National Guard but we must strike now before they flee across the border. We must go to the House of Dreams and we must go now. Mount up! We go to their house of death!'

Men surged towards the old man's truck. Juan turned away and went to where Luis and Angelina were standing with María by the front door.

(4)

Pablo drove east across the city towards the headquarters of the Brigadas Especiales. El Toro sat beside him in the cab, his carbine sticking out through the open window. Everywhere people were out on the streets celebrating. On seeing the fighters in the back of the truck they waved and cheered. 'Keep moving,' El Toro ordered.

Pablo said, 'Do you tell your wife how to cook?'

'Just drive,' snarled El Toro. Pablo looked at him in surprise. 'We need to get there before the rats leave the sinking ship,' he added. An awkward silence filled the cab. El Toro said, 'She's dead.' Pablo glanced across at him. 'My wife; she's dead.'

'I'm sorry. I hadn't heard.'

They drove on in silence. After a while El Toro said, 'I was not there when the Brigadas Especiales came. They were looking for me.' He lapsed into silence again. Then as if thinking aloud he said, 'I thought killing them would ease the pain.' The old man stole another glance at him. El Toro was looking straight ahead. 'They used to call me the gentle giant,' he said, 'now I am just El Toro and people fear me.'

'I don't fear you.'

El Toro gave him a bleak smile. It did little to change the expression on his face though his eyes seemed to come alive again. 'I know it, you old goat. It's why I like you.'

They were approaching the headquarters of the Brigadas Especiales. 'Stop here,' El Toro said, as the barrier came into view.

Pablo brought the truck to a stop. The men in the

back were all out before it had even come to a standstill. Addressing the men El Toro said, 'They may have fled already but equally they may be waiting for us. Follow me, fan out and keep your eyes open. And don't bunch up!'

Pablo watched them close in around the guardhouse. On El Toro's signal they opened fire. The glass in the windows shattered, splinters of wood flew in all directions and bullet holes appeared along the front of the whole building. Then, as the firing stopped, El Toro alone ran forward. He stood beside the door, his back to the wall before opening the door with his left hand and pushing it open. One of his men fired a short burst of automatic fire through the now open door. The moment it stopped El Toro burst into the room. He emerged a few seconds later saying, 'Nobody at home!'

The group moved on down the road towards the headquarters of the Brigadas Especiales. Pablo started the truck. Slowly he followed them as far as the junction where he sat and watched as El Toro entered the building. Some of his men waited beside the front door. Then after a minute or so they too entered the building. Leaving his truck, Pablo approached the much-feared headquarters of the Brigadas Especiales. Both the building and the street were unnaturally quiet. With difficulty he mounted the steps to the front door, pausing briefly by the sign which read 'Welcome to the House of Dreams'.

(5)

El Toro was coming down the curved staircase. Seeing Pablo he said, 'We are already too late. They've gone.'

Before Pablo had a chance to respond to this a young man appeared from a door on the ground floor. 'Comandante, you need to see this.'

El Toro and Pablo followed the young fighter towards the back of the building until they came to a door that opened out onto a small courtyard. As they emerged into the sunlight they became aware of an appalling smell. Then they saw the bodies. They were lying strewn about like so much grotesque rubbish. Men and women, some only partially clothed, they lay in the sun, flies buzzing around their bodies. The old man crossed himself. Their guide said, 'There are more. That door over there leads to the cells. They killed everyone before they left.'

Several of El Toro's men already in the courtyard stood looking at him. 'How many more are there?' he asked.

'About twenty at a guess. I'm sorry I didn't count them.' The young man's face was set.

'It's all right. I would not expect you to have done.' Then turning to Pablo he said, 'I am afraid we need your truck for this, old man.'

'I have had to take bodies to the mortuary before,' replied Pablo.

El Toro looked at him. 'I am sorry to hear it.' Then turning back to his men he said, 'We need to get these bodies to the city mortuary. Pablo will fetch his truck. Tomás you go with him.' A visibly relieved young man stepped forward. El Toro glanced at Pablo. The old man nodded and followed as Tomás led the way.

Then addressing his men El Toro said, 'I need volunteers to help me collect the bodies from the cells and load them onto Pablo's truck.' No one moved. The sun beat down indiscriminately upon the bodies of the living and the dead. El Toro waited. One by one his men slowly raised a hand signalling their willingness to help. El Toro stood looking at them. A bleak smile appeared on his lined face. He said, 'This is why we won; because we always did what had to be done. Now let us get this done too.'

(6)

The newly promoted Captain Guba showed Juan into the outer office of the administration building where Colonel Escobar stood waiting. For a few seconds the two men just looked at one another. Then Colonel Escobar said, 'My office was damaged recently but please have a seat.'

'I could not help noticing. Thank you Colonel.' Juan sat down. He said, 'If I may say so, Colonel, you seem to have acquired a rather spectacular view of the parade ground.'

'Spectacular,' Colonel Escobar savoured the word. 'Unusual perhaps but then we live in unusual times.'

'I agree,' said Juan. The two men sat looking at one another.

Sounds from the outside world drifted into the room. At length Colonel Escobar said, 'I have never before had the pleasure of meeting someone who claims to be able to speak on behalf of the Liberation Front.'

'Such a meeting has only recently become feasible, would you not agree Colonel?'

'It would have been difficult certainly,' conceded the colonel with a thin smile. He said, 'I understand that you are here to try and establish a protocol designed to ensure that fighting does not break out between my National Guard and fighters of the Liberation Front?'

'That is correct, Colonel.'

'And what do you propose?'

'To begin with, continued contact avoidance which you have already accomplished by tactical withdrawal.'

The colonel's body stiffened. The difference was subtle, the effect startling. 'Three Brigade has not made a tactical withdrawal. The sole purpose of their being withdrawn to barracks was to put an end to pointless bloodshed. That is a very different thing.'

'My apologies, Colonel. I must learn to choose my words more carefully.'

'That is always a good idea,' replied Colonel Escobar. Juan remained silent.

'Please continue,' invited the colonel.

Juan said, 'The Front does not wish to see the

National Guard disbanded, they are after all the national army but for the time being if it could be arranged that they respect the current curfew while lifting it for civilians and members of the Front that should ensure that the nights remain peaceful. Would you be willing to accept such an arrangement, Colonel?'

'Possibly,' replied Colonel Escobar, 'but let me hear what else you are suggesting.'

'Both sides need instant visual recognition of peaceful intention.'

'That presupposes that each trust the other, surely? Otherwise one could merely be attempting to lure the other into a trap.'

'With respect, Colonel, trust comes later and is built slowly on the basis of experience.'

'Agreed but in the meantime?'

'In the meantime, even as we speak, members of the Front are attempting to capture or kill all members of the Brigadas Especiales. Those that are taken prisoner will be held accountable for any crimes they have committed. The National Guard must refrain from any attempt to protect them.'

'The Front can rest assured no member of the Brigadas Especiales will be protected or aided by Three Brigade. In fact I shall instruct my men to take them prisoner or kill them. Those dogs have brought the whole of the army into disrepute.'

The colonel's demeanour left Juan in little doubt that

he would be as good as his word. He asked, 'Would you be prepared to hand over any such prisoners to the Front, Colonel?'

'I would,' replied Colonel Escobar.

'What about the rest of the army? I mean other than Three Brigade. Will they be prepared to do the same?'

'I cannot answer for them but I suspect you will find the Brigadas Especiales have few friends left. Most people who have seen death and suffering wish only to be able to get on with their lives. Soldiers are no different but in every walk of life one comes across a few,' he paused, 'and war tends to leave a legacy of hatred. To forget is hard; to forgive even harder.'

Juan said, 'Perhaps there are some things only God can forgive.'

Colonel Escobar slowly bared his teeth. It took Juan a moment to realise that the man was actually smiling. 'I think perhaps we should have this part of our conversation after the war has actually ended, don't you?'

Juan smiled too. 'You are right of course, Colonel. Excuse me.' Then after a pause, Juan asked, 'Do you know anything about the whereabouts of the president, Colonel?'

'No.'

'If he is still in the country the Liberation Front will also wish to put him on trial for numerous crimes.'

'I would regard that as a matter for the Liberation Front, who I assume will wish to form a new government.'

'That is the intention, Colonel, as is the restoration of the rule of law. We did not fight one tyranny merely to see another take its place.'

'I hope you succeed,' replied Colonel Escobar. 'This country has suffered enough.'

Shortly afterwards their meeting came to an end and Captain Guba was instructed to escort Juan to the main gates.

(7)

It was María who opened the door when Juan returned to the house of Luis and Angelina Rodrigo. 'Oh Juan! Thanks be to God. We were so afraid for you.'

'I told you it would be all right,' he replied with a grin.

'Come in,' she gave him a radiant smile. 'Angelina and Señor Rodrigo are in the garden. I do not know who was more scared for you. The three of us…' she raised her arms in a gesture of helplessness. 'They will be so pleased to see you. Come in. Come in.' Taking his hand, she led the way. Juan was reminded of the young woman who, after they had run the weapons through the roadblock, had laughed until the tears ran down her cheeks. Then he remembered the tears she had shed for the son of Luis and Angelina Rodrigo. Juan wondered briefly if he should tell them that Doctor Mendez was dead, he doubted that María would have done so, but he decided against it.

On entering the garden Angelina came forward and took his hands in hers and looking into his face said quietly, 'You are a good and brave man Juan. If something had happened to you, I don't think,' her eyes were moist and she left the thought unfinished. Wiping the corners of her eyes with a small lace handkerchief she said, 'But you're all right.'

'Yes, quite all right, Señora. Thank you.'

Luis Rodrigo came and stood beside his wife. He said, 'We are so proud to know you and this young woman too,' he added smiling at María.

Angelina said, 'Would you like something to drink, a whisky or a beer perhaps?'

'A beer would be nice, thank you,' replied Juan.

María said, 'Let me get that Señora.'

'Thank you María. You are a good girl but I have told you to stop calling me Señora. You are part of our family now. And you are certainly *not* our maid.'

After she had left the room to fetch his beer Angelina said, 'If Ramón were still alive both Luis and I would have been very happy to see María and our son married. Sadly that can no longer be but for the time being, at least, until she falls in love again, we feel almost as if we have gained a daughter. Does that make sense to you?'

'It most certainly does,' replied Juan, 'and I am not at all surprised to hear you say it. María's life has not been easy and she really loved your son. I know that because I saw her grief when it was most raw and if, or when, she ever falls in love again, you will not lose what you have found in each other, of that I am absolutely certain. She is one of the most loyal and trustworthy people I have ever come across.'

'And you Juan, what of you?' asked Angelina in a voice fraying at its edge. 'You have such a lovely smile but such sad eyes. Tell us about yourself.'

'There is little to tell, Señora,' replied Juan, 'but if my eyes are sad it is because of the war, which hopefully is all but over now. But such terrible things happen in war; war marks us all, does it not?'

That evening after they had eaten and Juan had told them about his meeting with Colonel Escobar, the four of them sat in the garden listening, as the brief dusk ushered in only the second night free from gunfire in over three years and the cicadas offered up their own anthem to peace.

CHAPTER TEN

(1)

Pablo Herendez, wearing a military uniform and as head of the hastily convened three-man court, sat facing Colonel Escobar. He said, 'Nothing we've heard here today amounts to a defence against the charges you face. We're only concerned with the fact that as the commanding officer of Three Brigade you must bear responsibility for the atrocities committed by the men under your command. Atrocities committed both before and during the war that has just ended. We do not need to cite individual cases because for years the army was guilty of countless crimes and therefore you bear responsibility for those crimes and must answer for them. Have you anything more you wish to say before sentence is passed?'

'Only this,' replied Colonel Escobar, 'the charge against me, as you have just summarised it, is incontestable because it contains a definition of guilt requiring no evidence beyond the assertion of that guilt. Therefore I don't propose to waste any more of my breath. This was not a trial, it was a farce.'

'Clever words won't save you from justice, Colonel. You may sit down, while I confer with my colleagues, before passing sentence.'

'I prefer to remain standing,' replied Colonel Escobar.

'Suit yourself,' retorted El Tigre with a thin smile. The Tiger of the Night turned first to the man on his left, who after the briefest of whispered exchanges, nodded. Pablo Herendez then turned to the man on his right, who also nodded. Then, looking at Colonel Escobar he said, 'You've been found guilty as charged. You'll therefore be taken from here to face a firing squad. The sentence will be carried out immediately. These proceedings are now over.'

One of the rebel fighters standing behind the colonel placed a hand on his arm. Turning towards the man Colonel Escobar said, 'I am quite capable of walking unaided, thank you.' The young man stepped back. His companions moved aside as Colonel Escobar walked towards the door at the back of the room.

Outside the sun glared down into the little courtyard. A single post had been newly driven into the ground in front of the far wall. Colonel Escobar walked to it and turned to face the men now standing in a group watching him.

El Tigre entered the courtyard followed by the man who had been sitting to his right and who now ordered the firing squad to form up. As the men began to move into place El Tigre said, 'Tie him to the post.' Nobody moved. 'Tie him to the post, I said!'

With obvious reluctance a young man walked towards Colonel Escobar carrying a length of rope. As he approached, their eyes met. Half under his breath the man said, 'I'm sorry, Colonel.'

'It's all right amigo. Do what you have to do.'

'No talking to the prisoner,' roared El Tigre.

Colonel Escobar looked up at the sky. As good a day to die as any other, he thought. He was glad he had never married. As far as he knew he had never fathered any children. Three Brigade had become his family and his life. He wondered what he would have done if he had lived long enough to retire. He found himself surprised that the thought had never occurred to him before. He felt the young man pull his arms together behind him as he tightened the rope around his wrists. Colonel Escobar thought briefly of his parents and of the one woman he had really loved, of the men he had killed and how God, if he existed, would judge his life.

'May God have mercy on you, Colonel,' The young man whispered. Colonel Escobar turned his head to look at him but the young man was already walking back to take his place in the firing squad.

'Take aim.' The men raised their guns. 'Fire!'

(2)

El Toro said, 'That bastard Pablo Herendez said you had no authority to make a deal with Colonel Escobar.'

'But everyone knows that by killing General Gomez and confining Three Brigade to barracks he effectively took them out of the war. It precipitated the final collapse of the regime and the flight of the president. The man saved countless lives.'

'I know, Juan. I know.'

'And Herendez just had him put up against a wall and shot!'

'The first I knew about it was when the junta issued a statement announcing that Colonel Escobar had been tried as a war criminal, found guilty and executed. It was all done so fast he was dead before most of us even knew he had been taken prisoner. Apparently they just picked him up off the street.'

'Is this what we fought for?' Juan said, looking up into El Toro's face. 'Is this what so many people gave their lives for?'

El Toro sat down opposite him. He had never seen Juan like this before; it was as if something had broken inside the man. El Toro did not understand but wondered why he felt such an acute sense of emptiness. Juan just sat there with his head in his hands. El Toro noticed that he had begun to tremble and then he saw the tears falling to the ground. Getting up he went and sat beside him placing one of his huge arms across Juan's shoulders.

For a while the two of them sat there, as out on the streets the crowds celebrated. El Toro thought about his wife and the many National Guardsmen he had killed and that he would not have hesitated to kill Colonel Escobar himself had the opportunity arisen but what Juan had said was true. Colonel Escobar had indeed helped shorten the war; too late for many, too late for his wife. Savagely El Toro pushed away his grief and wondered why he felt like a man who had suddenly lost his way.

(3)

Doctor Mendez stood before the priest. 'You must kneel to drink the blood of Christ, my son,' the priest said. He watched the man sink slowly to his knees. Juan looked into the chalice; it was less than half full. The man was kneeling looking up at him but to his horror Juan saw that it was not Doctor Mendez who looked back at him but the young National Guardsman he had shot in the Valley of Ghosts. He let out a cry of anguish; the chalice fell from his hands. Blood splashed onto his trousers and flowed across the floor. 'Oh no!' he cried. 'No!' He bent to pick up the chalice.

'Here, let me do that for you.'

Juan turned to look at the speaker. Colonel Escobar held the chalice out to him.

Juan sat up. He was fully awake, drenched in sweat and shaking uncontrollably. Swinging his legs off the bed he sat on its edge trying to blot out the memory of the young

National Guardsman and how he had died. He found himself sobbing and gasping for breath but gradually his body stopped shaking and he stopped crying. He looked at his watch. He had just decided that he would quietly pack his few things and leave before anyone was up and reached for the glass of water on the bedside table but somehow it slipped from his hand and fell to the floor where it broke, shattering the stillness. He cursed softly under his breath. Getting off the bed, he picked up the pieces of broken glass. He was just about to start dressing when there was a light knocking on the door and it began to open. Juan pulled the sheet around him as Angelina Rodrigo peered around the edge of the door. She said, 'Are you all right Juan? I'm afraid I could hear you.'

'Hear me?'

'You were crying out.'

'I'm sorry, I must have been dreaming or something. Did I wake everybody?'

'No; Luis is asleep and María would not have been able to hear you from her room but I was awake anyway. May I come in?'

'Yes, yes of course, come in.'

'Juan you look awful and you sounded,' Angelina paused, 'you sounded in such terrible distress.'

'I'm sorry. I think,' he paused, 'I think,' he said again, but left the sentence unfinished.

Angelina said, 'It's things that have happened, things you have seen isn't it?'

'Please, Señora, I cannot talk about this right now. I'm sorry.'

'It's all right Juan, we do not have to talk about anything you do not want to talk about. Would you like me to get you a drink?'

'No, thank you, Señora. Please do not trouble yourself. I'll be all right. I'll be on my way in the morning. It was just a bad dream, that's all. I think I must have been more upset about Colonel Escobar's death than I realised.'

'You cannot hold yourself responsible for the deeds of others Juan.'

'Oh, how I wish it were that simple, Señora. But please can we not speak about it. I'm sorry to have disturbed you and as I said I will be on my way in the morning.'

"Where will you go, Juan? You know you are welcome to stay as long as you wish. If you go, we will all miss you, especially María. You two seem very close.'

'We were comrades. In war one shares certain experiences that build a special bond but some things are best forgotten.'

'But that is not always possible is it Juan?'

'No Señora, there are some things it is impossible to forget, as we both know.'

'So where will you go?'

'There is a small seminary in the mountains where I will be able to stay. I need to leave the capital and some of the places,' he paused. 'You know what I mean.'

'You will come back to us, won't you Juan? Please promise me you will come back.'

'I promise you Señora, but I have said too many goodbyes. If you will allow me, I would prefer to slip away before everyone is awake. Just tell them I will be back.'

'You prefer to slip away, like a coyote.'

'Something like that, Señora. I have always rather liked coyotes, personally,' he added, with a semblance of his old smile.

'María may be upset.'

'She will understand, believe me. Your husband, he will not be offended, will he?'

'No. I will make him understand.'

'Gracias, Señora.'

'Then I will just say, vaya con Dios, Juan.'

'Vaya con Dios, Señora.'

(4)

Almost five years passed before Juan returned to the house of Luis and Angelina Rodrigo. Five years during which peace failed to return to the land of poets and dreamers because remnants of the previous regime had begun a vicious guerrilla campaign from across the border. Nevertheless, it was now peaceful within the capital and it was Angelina Rodrigo who heard the bell and came to the front door to answer it. For a moment she stood looking at the robed priest who stood at the foot of the steps smiling up at her. Then suddenly she recognised him, 'Juan! Juan is it really you?'

'I said I would return.'

'I didn't recognise you.' She stood looking into his face. 'But are you really?' she left the question unfinished.

'Yes, I'm a priest now,' he replied.

She came down the steps towards him. He took her hands in his. 'How are you, Angelina?'

'Oh Juan! Juan.' Tears were streaming down her face but they were tears of joy. 'It is so good to see you again and after all these years.' She wiped away the tears. 'We had begun to wonder if we would ever see you again.'

'Oh ye of little faith,' he chided her, smiling.

She smiled back; then said, 'I suppose I have to address you as Father now.' He laughed and Angelina realised that she had never heard him actually laugh before.

'That will not be necessary,' he said. 'I have not come as a priest but to visit friends. How are you? How is Luis? And María, is she still with you?'

'Luis has trouble walking now,' replied Angelina, 'but apart from that we're all well and yes, María is still with us. She's going to be married soon, but come in. María and Luis will be so pleased to see you; come in.' She led him through the house towards the garden saying, 'You arrived at a good time, we were all having coffee.' Angelina stepped aside as they entered the garden, saying, 'Look who has come to see us.'

Juan watched Luis and María look up. Luis, he noticed, had aged but María appeared much as he remembered her and leaping to her feet came running towards him but then stopped half way, unsure how she should behave towards a man wearing the robes of a priest. Laughing, he said, 'I'm only wearing this because it's all I have.'

'Oh, Juan!' María rushed forward and flung her arms around him, burying her face against his chest. 'Juan. Juan.' Like Angelina, her immediate reaction was to cry. 'Why did you stay away so long? How could you do that to us?'

Looking over her shoulder, Juan said, 'I must apologise for making the women in your life cry, Luis. I don't think I'm supposed to have this effect on people.' He noted the tiredness of Luis' smile.

María pulled away from him, saying, 'Oh, you!' It was only then as they stood looking at each other that he saw the change in her. It's in the eyes, he thought. Eyes that have seen too much, too much horror, too much suffering; knowing eyes like Angelina's, eyes that see beneath the surface of things. Beyond her, Luis was slowly getting to his feet. Juan said, 'Don't get up on my account, Luis.'

Moving towards him, María said, 'Oh, I'm so sorry, how thoughtless of me.'

'Don't fuss me young lady,' said Luis. She stood back. The two men stood looking at one another. 'I knew you'd come back,' Luis said. 'I just didn't know you'd be wearing fancy dress.' Juan laughed. 'Actually, I'm not at all surprised to see that you've become a priest,' Luis continued. 'The Church needs priests like you, our country needs men like you.'

'You humble me, Luis. I'm not even sure that I should be a priest, after some of the things I've done,' replied Juan.

'As far as I'm concerned young man, you fought evil when only fighting could save the innocent. You did what had to be done. I'm sure that the God you believe in, if He really exists, knows your worth.'

'Oh, He'll know, He will know that for all of us.'

'So, you really do believe. Well, I suppose, you would. I'm afraid I lost what little faith I had, during the war. Strange, you fought and found God, while I, who did nothing, lost the faith I had.'

'You didn't do nothing Luis,' Juan began, but Angelina interjected, saying, 'Luis, is this the way to greet an old and dear friend? Let's at least give the man a cup of coffee before we begin to examine the state of our souls.' Both men smiled.

Two good men, Angelina thought, I wish Ramón was here but even as the thought entered her mind she became aware of Juan's gaze.

'I'll get another cup,' María said, leaving to get it.

The three of them sat down and the garden sounds framed a silence none of them chose to break with speech.

When María returned with the cup for Juan, she stopped beside the bougainvillea that framed the archway leading from the house to the garden and just stood there looking at them.

'What is it?' asked Angelina.

'He really did bring something with him, didn't he?' she replied.

'Yes, he has,' agreed Angelina, smiling.

'What are you both talking about?' asked Juan.

'Don't you know?' María asked. Juan said nothing.

'You're a priest all right,' said Angelina.

(5)

The day was hot and white clouds drifted slowly by overhead. As he walked, Juan remembered the time when he and María had brought weapons into the city. How, before they had run the roadblock, they had sat looking down at the lake shimmering in the distance; a brief respite of peace before they learned that Ramón was dead; and he remembered María's grief and how she had begged him to allow her to kill Doctor Mendez. And he recalled the look of gratitude and pride on the faces of Luis and Angelina, when he agreed to conduct the marriage service of María to her future husband. He thought of the love of God, His mercy and the blessing of remembrance and forgetfulness; of human beings and their capacity for both kindness and cruelty. And he thought about his life before he had even met Luis and Angelina Rodrigo and how after the war he had eventually become a priest and of his life now as he walked beneath the sun.

As he approached the steps leading up to the church of Our Lady of Mercy he noticed a young family who were standing looking up at the church. The man, who was in a wheel chair, had his back to him but his wife and the little boy whom he judged to be about nine years old, were both looking at him as he approached.

'Do you need any help?' he asked.

The woman said, 'Thank you Father, that is very kind of you. We were wondering how we were going to manage.'

Juan turned to face the man who slowly turned his wheel chair to face him. Juan gasped.

'This is the man who saved my life, Jaime,' Miguel Hortez said. 'After I was wounded in the war, he carried me to the Río Lamento. If he had not done so, I would have died. You and your mother would have been alone. Say thank you to the Father.'

The little boy said, 'Thank you, Father.'

'And this is my wife, Manolita,' Miguel Hortez said.

The eyes that looked at Juan seemed to him to reflect all the suffering and sadness of the world but the voice that said, 'I am so pleased to meet you, Father,' was soft and gentle like a mother's voice to her child.

ACKNOWLEDGEMENTS

I would like to begin by expressing my profound gratitude to Mr Pat Cunningham for his suggestions, many of which I acted upon, and which resulted in a greatly improved novel but especially because even while he took the time to go through some sample pages of the manuscript, he was himself undergoing chemo therapy.

I owe a similar debt of gratitude to Mr Mike Snedeker whose unwavering moral compass, fine example and friendship helped me through some difficult times, while he too endured cancer's malignant endeavours.

I would also like to record the encouragement I received from Mrs Mignon Garrett, founder of the Pendragon Writers Circle, who never ceased to believe in this book and for years urged me to finish it, something I have at last managed to do, though sadly not before she had passed away.

And I would also like to thank the following;

Mr Ian Treglowan whose early comments, after I had begun to work on it again, resulted in a major rewrite involving Captain Miguel Hortez' survival, which fundamentally changed the books whole development and character.

Mr Mick Derbyshire whose observations regarding ballistics corrected a serious factual flaw which would otherwise have marred the narrative.

Mrs Sue Hasson, Mrs Jo Hunter, Mrs Judy Sanders, Mr and Mrs Chris Blount, my friend Slopey, Mr Michael Parnell, Mr Ken Hannaford, Mr Tony Cunliffe, Mr Mark Catton and our friend Muz, Mr Mike Jarvis and Mr Simon Fernley and my friends in Truro Waterstones.

Mrs Jocelyn Hobbs whose proofreading helped turn my grammatically illiterate offering into something ultimately publishable.

And my thanks of course go to everyone at T J International involved in the production of this book but in particular to Ms Hannah Vaughan and Ms Magda Pieta who oversaw the jacket design and supervised the various typeset amendments and all the actual pre-production work.

Finally, this list of acknowledgements is inevitably incomplete, so let me end by also thanking all my friends and well-wishers, among the dead as well as the living, not named above but whose invaluable support helped sustain me over the years. You know who you are; my grateful thanks to all of you. Thank you.

M R Barclay